THREE DAYS GRACE

INDIGORIVER
PUBLISHING

Three Days Grace

JEREMY BRADLEY-SILVERIO DONATO

CONTENT WARNING:

This novel contains references to child sexual abuse, which may be distressing for some readers.

Three Days Grace

Editors: Shelby Poulin, Stephanie Thompson
Cover and Interior Design: Emma Elzinga
Cover Photo: Manuel Bonadeo
Author Photograph: Hanoh Szpira

Indigo River Publishing
3 West Garden Street, Ste. 718
Pensacola, FL 32502

www.indigoriverpublishing.com

Ordering Information:

Quantity Sales: Special discounts are available on quantity purchases by corporations, associations, and others. For details, contact the publisher at the address above.

Orders by US trade bookstores and wholesalers: Please contact the publisher at the address above.

Printed in the United States of America

Library of Congress Control Number: 2025927377
ISBN: 978-1-969935-20-6 (paperback) 978-1-969935-21-3 (ebook)

First Edition

To Les, Kris, and Jen:

Your support kept me going.

Your feedback made me better.

Your words gave me courage.

"Some things are too terrible to grasp at once."

– Donna Tartt, *The Secret History*

"It's like he loved doing it, like he wanted to make a little wound that would last forever."

– Siri Hustvedt, *What I Loved*

One

1.

Nick, frozen in the gathering dusk of his cramped Parisian room, perched on the edge of his chair in nothing but glacier-white briefs. The necessity of switching on a light loomed over him like an unwelcome task, as did the prospect of finishing getting dressed. He bargained with himself: five more minutes to linger in this liminal space as shadows stretched across the floorboards. His gaze drifted to his phone, lying face down on the table like a reproach. When he finally checked the time, the numbers jolted him to his feet.

He'd be late. The metro, with its warren of delays and disruptions, couldn't be trusted, and an Uber—even if he could justify the expense—would crawl through the city's glutted arteries. Such luxuries had become foreign to him anyway, casualties of his decision to "do what he really loved," a phrase that now carried a bitter aftertaste. He had no choice but to walk the two kilometers to the hotel, where his mother, Lynne, and her wife, Susan, waited.

Tomorrow, Lynne and Susan would board a plane to South Africa. Paris served merely as a comma in their journey from the States, barely worth noting. Despite a carefully timed and early departure from the office, Nick had squandered the precious minutes daydreaming, dreams which were as tangible as the bruises he'd long ago learned to hide, dreams with blurred edges like the old photograph on the dresser of him, his mother, and a third face now gone.

Nick hurried to the bathroom where his chosen armor lay in wait: black jeans and a black turtleneck, carefully arranged like a specter given form. These weren't his showiest pieces, but they carried quality in their very fibers. The kind of quality that whispered rather than shouted. He'd adopted the Parisian head-to-toe black as naturally as breathing, telling himself the uniform was cultural assimilation rather than camouflage. But didn't every transplant to the city do the same thing—wrap themselves in darkness like a protective spell?

Tonight's choice of the turtleneck felt different though—less shield, more weapon. Nick knew his mother Lynne would read its worth instantly, even without a designer's name screaming from the fabric. She would see the liquid way the material draped, how it caught the light like oil on water. The silk-cashmere blend settled against his skin with the weight of intention. *Look what I can afford without you*, the garment seemed to say. *Look what I've become despite everything*. Every thread morphed into a small rebellion, every perfect stitch a reminder that he'd built this life—even if it wasn't necessarily "the dream"—without her help, without her connections, without her giving a damn.

But the turtleneck couldn't hide what he really was: still her son, still wanting her to notice. "To hell with it," he muttered to his reflection, but the words fell as flat as his conviction.

Fog rose outside the windows as Nick moved through his apartment. He left a light burning as a beacon for his future self. He could almost believe the dinner was already over, that he was returning home to this waiting warmth, relieved by the knowledge that once Lynne and Susan's plane lifted off, he could pack away thoughts of his mother and her lover like winter clothes in summer. Their meetings were scattered so thinly across the calendar that each one felt like both beginning and ending, hello and goodbye compressed into the same breath.

The January air bit with midwinter teeth, but Nick wore only a threadbare overcoat, its stains and wear an obvious mismatch against the refined elegance beneath. The coat served as a sartorial contradiction, undermining the turtleneck's silent boast. Walking as fast as he could, Nick remembered that Marc would be there tonight, his mother's best friend and a true Parisian whose authenticity made Nick's adopted city-self feel like a poor translation. And then there was the artist. Susan had mentioned him in her last text message, along with her usual reminder that Lynne would love to hear from him more often, a face that flickered at the edges of Nick's memory like a candle about to burn out. The name Laslo echoed in Nick's mind as a faint trace from childhood, most details erased by time or willful forgetting.

As he hurried down the street, an approaching bus drew him into a sprint, and something electric sparked in his chest—a sudden, startling joy. The usual unreliability of Paris public transport made this timing magical, as if his desperate footsteps had conjured the vehicle from the gathering dark. For a moment, he almost turned to share the small victory with the ghost of someone long gone. But the impulse died as quickly as it came, leaving his nervous anticipation to transform into something like delight—the kind of miracle that made even the most anxious evening feel touched by fate.

2.

Across the Seine, in a weathered Haussmannian building near Saint-Sulpice, Marc lingered by his sink, contemplating an oversized glass of red wine he couldn't bring himself to want. The burgundy tasted more like duty than indulgence. With a gesture more decisive than careful, he set the wine down too hard, watching both liquid and glass shudder like a ship run aground. The glass slowly settled among the archipelago of unwashed dishes.

He retreated to his closet, where a wall of dark Mahogany loomed with its burden of clothing. The wardrobe exhaled its familiar musty breath as he reached in and extracted a blazer from its depths. As he shrugged it on, the weight of the evening ahead settled across his shoulders along with the fabric. Marc came from an old family, the kind whose pedigree was more curse than blessing. The generations of wealth had dwindled to almost nothing upon reaching him, leaving only the burden of appearances. He lived alone in the crumbling apartment he'd inherited from his grandmother, its faded grandeur a perfect metaphor for his life. The parquet floors creaked under his feet, the wallpaper peeled in corners, and even though Marc knew the place was falling apart, he did almost nothing to ever tidy up. He let disorder match the apartment's decline, like for like. So he compensated for his financial insecurity with elegance: tailored suits, silk scarves, and gifts—always tasteful, always expensive-looking—that he'd painstakingly source from secondhand stores, estate sales, and shops marked down half-price.

Marc stared at his phone where it lay in the crumpled bedsheets, the screen's glow an invitation to escape. The pandemic had given everyone a perfect excuse, hadn't it? Illness had become both more believable and more terrifying, a get-out-of-jail-free card that carried its own weight of anxiety. But this was Lynne, who had known him for more than twenty years, since they were colleagues in the States, when they'd shared cigarettes and secrets in dim faculty lounge corners. She didn't just ask how you were—she followed up with questions about your white blood cell count and whether your cough was productive. Calling in sick to Lynne meant preparing a dossier: symptoms listed in chronological order, doctor's credentials, medications and dosages cross-referenced with side effects. She wasn't nosy so much as pathologically thorough. And because she wielded that precision like a virtue, lying to her wasn't like lying to anyone else—it required a narrative architecture Marc no longer had the stamina to build.

He knew exactly what Lynne would say.

"Fuck off!" The words burst from him in perfect mimicry of her world-weary drawl, all wounded exhaustion and brittle disappointment, echoing off the walls of his chaotic flat. His own laughter surprised him—a flash of mellowness in the cool air. The moment of levity propelled him through the motions: hat settled just so, scarf wrapped with practiced elegance, peacoat buttoned against the evening chill. He descended the stairs with determination and stepped onto the street, where the looming omen of a black Mercedes taxi waited.

But as the leather seat embraced him, Marc's temporary spark of energy guttered and died. He mumbled the hotel's address in a voice heavy with resignation, then retreated into silence. Even the driver—a young North African with the kind of handsomeness that would normally have sparked Marc's interest—couldn't draw him from his deepening gloom. The young man's attempts at conversation dissolved into the space between them, unanswered. Anyway, Marc had always believed that traffic-heavy rides across town were a chance for reflection.

He tried to remember the first time he'd met Lynne all those years ago during his stint teaching French literature at, what he called, a *médiocre* American university. Lynne had been the quiet anchor of the humanities faculty. She had been respected but not flashy, with a dry sense of humor that Marc had immediately liked. She, in turn, found his wit and old-world charm amusing. Her intelligence had always struck him—the relentless way she filled the air with words, and the uncanny way she could puncture tension with a single, well-placed line. At the same time, Americans had the tendency, Marc had always thought, to overshare, and so their conversations often drifted into the personal. During one of these chats, Lynne had admitted, almost offhandedly, that her marriage felt "complicated." Though Marc had wanted to pry, he had simply nodded, offering her the kind of unspoken understanding that he himself often craved.

Now, decades later, his connection to Lynne remained one of the few threads linking him to a past that sometimes seemed more imagined than real. The only true friend he had: The one he'd call when something happened, when something was (rarely) worth sharing, and the only one he'd meet at the drop of a hat, booking last-minute trips to Rome or Istanbul or Reykjavik on his American Express card. The one who had left her husband for Susan, who'd also been their colleague at the university. Susan had been the department's rising star, he remembered, full of ambition and ideas that sometimes grated on her older colleagues.

But Lynne was indispensable to Marc, not only because of their shared history. She had the uncanny ability to see through his layers of artifice. While others might have admired his tailored suits and affectations, Lynne saw past the curated exterior to the person underneath. She never voiced her observations, but in her crisp remarks and knowing glances, Marc could tell she understood just how threadbare his world had become. That awareness both comforted and unsettled him; Lynne's presence was a quiet reminder of the truths he preferred to ignore: That he wasn't as refined as he liked to appear, and not nearly as successful—or as happy—as he wanted others to believe.

Tonight, though, the thought of seeing Lynne, and by extension Susan, brought a mix of dread and relief. He'd spent too many nights alone recently, sipping wine he couldn't afford and scrolling aimlessly through his phone. The thought of sharing even a fraction of his burden—of hearing Lynne's sardonic yet oddly grounding voice—almost made him forget how exhausting her company could be. As the car slipped through the streets of Paris, Marc closed his eyes and tried to summon the energy.

3.

Laslo hunched over the desk in his drab studio, a stub of pencil pinched between his fingers as he marked another passage in his well-worn textbook on light and tonality. His fingers moved with lupine precision, stalked across the yellowed pages, paused to circle a phrase here, underline a principle there—a manuscript he returned to as his secular prayer book whenever inspiration ran dry. The thought of leaving tugged at him, and he lifted his eyes to the enormous windows that dominated the space. Below, the Bateaux Mouches, shapes softened by the gathering fog, carved their patient paths through the Seine.

A flicker of concern passed through Laslo at the sight of the heavy sky. He'd forgotten his umbrella that morning, and the threat of rain hung in the air like one of his many unfinished paintings. But the worry remained performative, almost amusing. After all, what kind of self-proclaimed bohemian fretted about umbrellas and weather forecasts? Such mundane concerns were meant for others, not for someone who'd made an art form of affected carelessness.

Laslo gathered his outer layers and began the descent, each of the five flights of stairs creaking beneath his feet. Outside, the fog had swallowed the tourist boats whole, leaving the Seine a blank canvas of white and grey. He stood motionless before the building. The day had somehow slipped through his fingers without leaving so much as a fingerprint. The unsettling feeling held him there like an invisible anchor until thoughts of Susan surfaced in his mind, memories that propelled him toward the metro entrance glowing at the corner.

Laslo had met Susan and Lynne during a brief but formative year abroad in the United States. He had arrived with an unshakable confidence in his aesthetic sensibilities, ready to be unimpressed by what he imagined would be a dull, Midwestern campus. But instead, he found himself captivated—not by the university itself, with its sprawling brick buildings and painfully manicured lawns, but by the vibrant, messy world within. As the department's visiting artist, he'd been immediately drawn into their tight-knit academic circle and spent nearly every evening at faculty gatherings. Laslo had become an almost daily fixture in their lives.

Susan had been the first to take him under her wing, though her interest had come across almost scientific, as if she were trying to prove something to and about herself. At a humanities department mixer, her hand had shot out in an assertive handshake that felt more like a challenge than a greeting. "Laslo, right? The graduate exchange student from Paris?" she had said, her accent clipped and precise. Her tall, wiry energy kept her perpetually in motion, even when standing still. She had a penchant for slightly too-large men's blazers, which she wore over band t-shirts, her style veering somewhere between academic and punk.

Then Susan had introduced him to Lynne, a colleague in the same department but strikingly different in demeanor. Lynne moved through the world with a watchful intensity that reminded Laslo of the way one is meant to study a painting: not just looking but dissecting, interpreting. Lynne had been married at the time, a detail Susan divulged and then dismissed with offhand irritation. But even from their first encounter, Laslo had sensed the electric undercurrent between the two women.

The tension revealed itself in small moments: the way Lynne's eyes lingered on Susan's hands as the younger woman gestured, the way Susan's voice softened—ever so slightly—when addressing Lynne. Laslo had a knack for observing the spaces between people, for noting the unspoken, and in the weeks that followed, he began to assemble their story. He'd notice how Lynne's tone would sharpen when speaking about her husband, the mere sound of his name scraping raw against her nerves. He'd catch Susan stealing glances at Lynne during faculty meetings, the look on her face somewhere between amusement and longing.

One evening, after a gallery opening that had been more pretentious than inspiring, the three of them had ended up at a dive bar on the edge of campus. Lynne's cheeks were flushed from the wine, and Susan animatedly recounted a story about a disastrous attempt to teach an undergraduate class on abstract expressionism. Laslo sat back, his drink untouched, and watched as Lynne leaned closer to Susan, their laughter mingling in a way that felt conspiratorial. He had seen this kind of connection before, in the couples who wandered the banks of the Seine in Paris, his adopted home, or in the way his parents looked at each other back in his native Hungary. The signs blazed as unmistakable as sunlight.

"You're quiet tonight," Susan had remarked, fixing Laslo with a pointed look. "What's going on in that brain of yours?"

"Just taking it all in," Laslo had said, the corners of his mouth lifting in something too sharp to be called a smile.

He never asked directly about their relationship; he wouldn't have wanted to disturb the rhythm of those months. Susan had been playing at getting him into bed—dropping flirty comments in department meetings, tucking little notes into his cubby hole. They were all like that then, curious about love and comfort and feeling. They had both understood their roles in the performance: her cultivating an acceptable crush while her real desire lay elsewhere, him providing the perfect cover for her lingering gazes at faculty gatherings. By spring semester, the pretense had worn thin, but they maintained the illusion anyway, a comfortable fiction that protected deeper truths. After Lynne's husband had left and Lynne had moved in with Susan, the pieces clicked into place. By then, Laslo's time in Missouri had become a memory, a chapter in his life defined by long conversations, fleeting connections, and the quiet revelation of things left unsaid. Things that fueled his creativity.

The years since he'd last seen Susan had blurred together, marked only by the lengthy text exchanges that she often initiated. Antipathy hadn't kept him from reaching out—rather, their dynamic had crystallized this way years ago: Susan pursuing, Laslo receiving. The pattern had begun in their younger days, when her passion for him burned fierce and bright, before she discovered—or rather acknowledged, he corrected himself—that she preferred women. Even then, they had shared secrets, late-night confessions traded like contraband. But after her coming out, something in their connection deepened and clarified. The flirtation evaporated, and in its place came a rawer, steadier intimacy: less charged, perhaps, but more expansive. They began talking not just about feeling but about frameworks—family wounds, personal myths, the psychic sediment of old desires. Susan had become Laslo's confidante and occasional provocateur, his source of inspiration when academic jargon and aesthetic philosophy couldn't suffice.

Their recent exchanges, though, had taken on a heftier tone. The usual secret-sharing was replaced by Susan's raw dispatches from the frontlines of Lynne's battles with the bottle. But inevitably, the storm clouds would part, and they'd fall back into an easy familiarity, often discussing Nick, Lynne's son who'd made Paris his home. "*Our* son," Susan would call him, and the yearning in the words made Laslo wince. That possessive "our" hung in their conversations as a note held too long. From what Laslo could remember, Susan had never wanted children, and as it were, Nick was twenty-eight and hardly in need of a second mother. So tonight would be a reunion, he thought: of people, of ideas, of things left unspoken. And that excited him.

4.

In the hotel bathroom, Susan's hair snagged in the straightening iron, the strands blooming red as they burned. The clicking noise of the device provided thin cover for Lynne's voice, which seeped through the door's expensive wood like smoke. Soon, Susan would have to emerge and face her wife in the bedroom. She switched the iron off, then immediately back on, her jaw clenched tight enough to ache. The morning's breakfast drama still festered. Lynne refused to let the issue go, in the same way that she refused to let all little things go but ignored the big ones. But Susan hadn't been wrong about that waiter, the way his hovering presence had practically demanded a tip. It wasn't their fault he failed to realize that they knew Paris, that they understood tipping wasn't customary here.

"You made us look like ignorant tourists," Lynne's voice cut through the closed door, "and worse, like cheap ones. Susan? Susan, I know you can hear me! How could you hesitate over a simple tip? Do you have any idea what servers make in places like that? And it's not even about the money—we looked cheap."

Susan, having freed her hair from earlier, now held the straightener too long in another spot, the strands beginning to smell singed. But paralysis gripped her. She couldn't bring herself to move.

Lynne's lecture continued its relentless flow: "You know how Marc handles these things? He's a real Parisian. Always keeps a five euro note ready, leaves it right there on the table. When the card machine asks for a tip, he hits ten percent without thinking twice. He tells me these waiters live dreary lives, catching night buses home after their shifts, all the way out to the suburbs because the city's priced them out."

Susan finally emerged from the bathroom, offering Lynne a placating smile—one Susan had perfected over the years. "Yes, you're right." The simple admission of guilt worked its usual magic on Lynne, deflating her indignation like a punctured balloon.

Lynne seized the opportunity to change course. "Look at the time! Everyone will be here any minute. Though I won't hold it against Laslo if he's late. He's a real struggling artist, your precious Laslo. Not so different from those waiters, come to think of it, the same ones you're so concerned about when it's someone else doing the stiffing."

The window had been left open, and all at once, a downpour began, blowing the curtains into the room. Lynne moved to the window and observed the scene below: wipers keeping their desperate rhythm across taxi windscreens, traffic lights bleeding crimson through the rain's veil, the asphalt transformed into a black mirror by the deluge. Somewhere in that watery chaos, Nick pushed forward, making his way to them. The idea settled in her stomach like a cold weight. The feeling wasn't dread, not quite guilt, just the heavy recognition of another scene in a play that she'd stopped directing years ago.

Lynne's fingers reached into her pocket and found her phone. She checked for messages, though she'd have heard any notification. The petty drama with Susan had been nothing—just another small cruelty in a world full of them—but the quarrel had wound her nerves so tight that her hands trembled as they clutched the device. In truth, a deeper hurt had Lynne on edge.

The news had arrived during their morning café squabble. Susan had been tapping her card on the machine with no success when Lynne's phone lit up. Later, Lynne would remember every detail of that moment with brutal clarity: the waiter shifting his weight, trying to hide his impatience with Susan's inability to simply push a button and leave a tip, the bitter smell of coffee grounds and warm croissants, the morning light catching the zinc bar just so, the way her hands nearly gave out as she read Kate's message about her ex-husband Gene.

"Who is it?" Susan had asked, finally managing to pay the bill. Lynne heard herself answer as if from a great distance. Her voice was too bright, too brittle: "Oh, just Nick asking for directions." But her eyes kept returning to those stark words on the screen: heart attack, died in his sleep, funeral arrangements. "Get me a Tylenol," she managed, then, desperate to focus on anything else: "You were so rude to that waiter, you know." And so began their argument about tipping, about cultural differences, about anything except the truth burning in Lynne's pocket. Gene had died.

As Susan excavated two aspirins from her purse, Lynne returned to her phone and unconsciously narrated as she typed—a habit she'd never broken: "I'll call you in the morning."

Susan's brow furrowed. "Call Nick? But he's coming to the hotel tonight, isn't he?"

Lynne had let Susan's question dissolve into silence, and Susan, sensing something, hadn't pushed.

Presently, something fierce and inexorable took over Lynne's mind like a fever: the exhausting prospect of performing motherhood for a son she'd never learned how to talk to, of pretending there was still something to salvage from the wreckage of their non-relationship. But conversely, she felt an almost delirious satisfaction that among all those they'd be with tonight, she carried this weighty secret. Lynne had always loved the control that came with the clandestine. Gene's death stood solid and consequential amid the day's arguments over tips, dinner plans, and travel logistics. For a heartbeat, she wondered if this news would derail their carefully planned journey. But no, she dismissed the nearly-formed thought. She couldn't allow death, even this death, to claim such power. Lynne had never let death do that—even when it had mattered most.

Across the room, Susan, eyeing the minibar, wondered if Lynne had been sneaking drinks the entire time she'd been in the bathroom messing with her hair. Still, Susan offered Lynne another smile, ignoring the tender spots along her hairline where the iron had kissed too close.

"Earlier," Lynne ventured, "did you remember to tip the bellboy for the bags?"

"Of course I did, love," Susan lied with practiced ease and then gestured toward the window. She was desperate to shift topics. "It's really coming down." And then, catching herself in the window's reflection: "My hair is a disaster."

Lynne, ignoring the comment, moved toward the minibar's promise of relief. A knock came at the door, and Susan moved to answer.

"Am I first?" Nick asked, his gaze sliding past Susan to find his mother. Susan's carefully constructed smile—her third in as many minutes—hung abandoned on her face.

"Hello," Lynne breathed, the word emerging as an aria, a performance Nick knew he could never match. His own greeting would be dust against her grandeur, so he opted instead for the physical, leaning in for a hug.

His mother wrapped him in a fierce but brief embrace before retreating to the minibar.

"Isn't he handsome?" Lynne said to Susan. "You must be fighting off men in the streets?"

And so the production had begun. Lynne surprised herself at how quickly she rose to the occasion—muscle memory from years of social theater, the ability to slip into maternal pride as easily as pulling on a well-worn coat. Nick's embrace had carried its own message—deliberate, calculated. A touch that could be given or taken away. They were both playing their parts now, mother and son, each move choreographed by old wounds.

"What do you want to drink, Nick?" Susan asked, her face now blank.

"Just water. *De l'eau plate.*" Nick caught himself in his French and wondered why he'd spoken that way, to two Americans, his so-called family. He blamed nerves and waited for the familiar pattern to establish itself—for Susan and Lynne to fall into their usual rhythm, a dance that left him in their comfortable shadow. These first moments always crackled with unnamed tension, an inexplicable sense of threat he could never quite articulate.

He hadn't lived with his mother since age fifteen. That's the problem, he told himself. They were forever starting from the moment he'd moved away.

But even this explanation fell flat. Between him and Lynne lay not emptiness, but something alive and wounded. "I've always tried to be a good mother, even if I wasn't," she loved to declare.

"How are you, my boy?" Lynne asked now, gin and tonic in hand as she posed against the windowsill.

Nick did not respond, instead taking a seat on the first available surface. He hoped they'd continue doing whatever they were doing, so he took out his phone and played around, opening apps, closing them, opening the same ones again.

But another reason kept Nick from looking in his mother's direction—he didn't want to shatter the illusion that he was more successful than she might believe. Wrapped in his fine turtleneck and constantly checking his phone for "important messages," he clung to that mirage like a performer holding his pose until the curtain falls. He held this fragile, furtive hope as if its survival depended on his silence, on his refusal to turn. As long as he maintained the pretense, she might step behind him, press her palms over his eyes, and sing out, *Guess who?*—and for a fleeting moment, he'd be a child again. Back when everything carried the fantasy of being whole, unbroken. Back when there were two boys for her to love, before silence became the only answer to questions too painful to ask. The longer he resisted turning, the longer he avoided answering her simple question, the more vivid her presence became. With each moment, her breath grazed nearer the back of his neck, drawing closer.

Something about waiting, the act of hoping without betraying the slightest sign of expectation, enthralled him. As if by refusing to acknowledge her watching, her waiting, he could somehow bargain with fate itself. Because life, he knew, seldom grants us what we want most. He had known others who had learned that lesson differently, choosing absence over endurance. And yet, perversely, he played at forgetting this truth—courting fortune's favor in the only way he knew: by pretending not to care, trusting that the moment he surrendered to despair, life might, at last, relent.

But Lynne had moved on: "Don't you wish Nick could join us in Cape Town, Susan? Susan, he asked for still water, not sparkling."

"Was it still or sparkling?" Susan called back.

"Either's fine," Nick muttered. "Whatever's easier."

"But you said still," Lynne pressed.

"I did say still, but honestly, it doesn't matter."

"Are you sure, Nick?"

Hope, then doubt. Nick thought he'd cracked his mother's game—seen through her strategy, anticipated her next move.

But then, just as certainty had settled, disbelief crept back. In limbo, Nick scrambled for an approach. Should he conceal his advantage? Flaunt the expensive cashmere? Appear absorbed in work? Or signal, with meticulous precision, that she had his full and undivided attention? Lynne was his mother. This should have been an easy game to master.

Then, in an instant, the illusion shattered. It wasn't her, at least not the version he had prepared for. She was shifting, dissolving into something new, unfamiliar. Every time he saw her, she became someone else. He wondered how much of this metamorphosis was Susan's doing, how much was alcohol, and how much was the vague and slippery notion of "authenticity," whatever that means. Or maybe the answer was some twisted combination, braided together into a version of his mother he no longer recognized.

"Never mind," Nick said, reaching for the sparkling water.

"I can fix a new one," Susan offered, as if pouring water required real effort.

To Nick, the lilt in Susan's voice felt almost like mockery—light, but intentional—as if she were amused by how easily she could disrupt his composure while pretending to be nice.

Her smile lingered, ambiguous. Was she reinforcing her boldness or hinting that she doubted Nick's unaffected demeanor? He couldn't be sure.

"I said, 'don't you wish Nick could join us in Cape Town, Susan,'" Lynne repeated from across the room. "It would almost be like being whole again."

Silence rose between them as abruptly as a held breath before a confession. Clearly, no one had anything to say. The little game of *still* versus *sparkling* water had become a stand-in for conversation, a way to pass time when no suitable subject presented itself.

Someone knocked at the door.

"Oh, Christ," Lynne said, her tone a little too forced. "That must be Marc. I was hoping for a moment with just the three of us, but..."

In Marc's place stood a man whose jaw disappeared beneath a thicket of hair as wiry and aggressive as hackles.

"Hello, darlings," Laslo announced to the room at large, his voice carrying a warmth that didn't quite reach his eyes. Nick noticed how the man's dark pupils darted around the room. Laslo was taking quick inventory of everyone's drinks, positions, and the subtle hierarchies of who sat where.

"Look who's here, Su," Lynne cooed, offering her cheeks for the ritual French *bisous.*

Nick watched as Laslo performed the greeting with seasoned poise, noting how the artist's hand lingered a fraction too long on Susan's waist. Everything about Laslo appeared calculated, from his rumpled blazer to his timed arrival.

Laslo crossed straight to Nick. Nick met Laslo's handshake, a theatrical parody of American warmth, and recognized the ironic performance in the gesture. A flash of understanding passed between them. They were both caught in Lynne and Susan's orbit, both playing their assigned roles. The handshake held a beat too long, like a private joke, but Nick couldn't shake the feeling that Laslo was measuring him, cataloging his weaknesses with the same clinical attention he'd given the room.

"I brought wine," Laslo announced, producing a bottle from his coat. He'd chosen carefully: a brand not expensive enough to show off, but good enough to prove he knew what he was doing. Nick studied the label—a boutique Bordeaux that he knew would impress Susan without intimidating her. Laslo apparently paid careful attention to his friends, built a dossier of their preferences, stored away details for future use.

"Though I see you've started without me." He nodded at Lynne's gin and tonic. His tone remained light, but something wolfish lurked in the way he observed her slight intoxication and the looseness of her laugh.

Laslo prowled through the room with the confidence of someone who had mapped every exit and then settled into the empty chair beside Susan—the best vantage point from which to observe everyone else.

"The rain caught me on the way," Laslo said, running a hand through his damp hair. "I had to duck into a doorway near Odéon. Quite romantic, really, watching all the umbrellas on the street." He spoke to the room, but his eyes kept returning to Susan, searching her face for something—recognition, perhaps, or the ghosts of their shared past.

"Marc's running late," Lynne announced, though no one had asked. "He just texted. Something about his taxi getting stuck in traffic in Saint-Germain." Straightening things that didn't need straightening, she moved around the room with nervous energy. The news of Gene's death rattled beneath her movements, though only she felt its vibration.

"Traffic's brutal in this weather," Nick offered, grateful for a neutral topic. "I almost took an Uber myself, but…" He trailed off, not wanting to mention money.

"Public transport is more authentic anyway," Laslo said, rescuing him. "Speaking of authenticity—Susan, are you still lecturing in Missouri? All those earnest Midwestern faces hanging on your every word about the French?" Warmth belied his teasing, but Susan's smile tightened.

"I'm on sabbatical," she said, topping up Nick's glass of water—again sparkling, though no one corrected her. "Writing a book about Colette's artistic circle. Or trying to." Her eyes flicked over to Lynne, who performed an elaborate ritual with ice cubes at the minibar.

"A book!" Laslo exclaimed. "How wonderful." He spoke with studied, formal English, as if aristocratic affectation could paper over his Hungarian origins and piss poor French. The roughness showed through anyway. "Though I always thought Colette was better at living than being written about," he said. "Remember that café near the Palais Royal where they say she used to write? It is still there, though it's full of tourists now. Lynne, darling, what are you constructing over there?"

"Just getting everything ready," Lynne said, her voice pitched too high. "We should open Laslo's wine. But damn it, there's no corkscrew here. What a hotel… Nick, get the corkscrew from my bag. The small blue one."

Nick moved toward the neat stack of luggage in the corner of the hotel room and wondered if his mother had ever packed a corkscrew on any trip. Still, he searched, keeping up the pretense. Something had her on edge tonight, more than usual.

As Nick rummaged through his mother's bag, he took in the room's attempts at old-world glamour. Everything mimicked Ritz standards: the moldings fell just short of ornate, the chandelier sparkled like crystal but didn't quite shine, the carpet teased at luxury without letting feet sink in. The room echoed of somewhere more expensive you'd once stayed, or could imagine staying. Heavy cream curtains framed the drizzle-streaked windows, and a few generic oil paintings of Parisian rooftops hung at carefully calculated intervals.

"Never mind the corkscrew," Lynne waved her hand. "I'm sure we can call down for one. Though they'll probably charge us twenty euros for the service." She laughed, but her voice faltered. "Laslo, tell us about your new work. The light studies?"

"Oh, God, no." Spreading his legs with effortless ease, Laslo sank deeper into one of the faux-Louis XVI chairs. "No one wants to hear about that," he added, though he was lying—he was always eager to talk about his work. Instead, he leaned forward. "Tell me about Cape Town. How long will you be there? Susan mentioned something about a beach house?"

"Three weeks," Susan answered, half-perched on the arm of the sofa, unwilling to commit to staying. "Lynne's sister Julia has a place in Camps Bay. She's letting us—"

A sharp knock cut through the room, this time inevitably belonging to Marc.

"Finally!" Lynne exhaled with relief at the arrival of her best friend. "Now we're all here. Well, almost." She hesitated, stealing a glance at Nick before shifting her focus elsewhere. The absence edged its way between them, unspoken but undeniable.

Lynne pulled open the door, her greeting dismissing Susan's questioning look. "Marc! You're late!"

Marc stood in the doorway, like an actor stepping into a scene he hadn't rehearsed. Rain had soaked his blazer at the shoulders, but he wore an unbothered smile. In one hand, he held a bottle of Gevrey-Chambertin; in the other, an unopened umbrella, a detail that made Nick grin despite himself.

"Traffic was impossible," Marc announced, stepping into the room and taking in the assembled group with a sweep of his eyes that lingered a second too long on Nick. "But what a lovely room! Very..." he paused, searching for the right word, "...diplomatic."

"Isn't it?" Lynne latched onto the comment. "Though they've put us on the wrong side. I specifically asked for a view of the Tuileries. But then, at these rates…" She let the sentence dangle.

Susan continued to watch Lynne, the terse moment between mother and son hanging in the air like cigarette smoke in an old photograph. But Lynne had already moved on, orchestrating the reorganization of glasses and seating arrangements with the intensity of someone directing traffic.

"Well, now that everyone's here," Lynne raised her voice, "shall we think about dinner? I've made a reservation at that place near Place des Vosges—the one you mentioned, Marc?"

"Ah, yes," Marc nodded, still standing with his unopened wine. "Though in this rain…"

"We could stay here," Susan suggested. "Order room service. The restaurant downstairs looked—"

"No, no," Lynne cut in. "It's our only night all together. Nick, my boy, you know the place I mean? The one with the little courtyard?"

Nick shifted. "I think so. If it's the one you mentioned, it's more Bastille than Vosges."

"Bastille, Vosges, what's the difference?" Laslo waved his hand. "It's all the same *arrondissement*. Though I must say, the rain makes everything feel rather far." He observed the dynamic between Lynne and Nick with the interest of someone studying a complex game.

Raindrops streaming like veins over the windows, the room had grown warm and close, a cocoon of forced intimacy. Lynne paced between the minibar and the window, smoothed the pleats of her skirt, folded them down again and again. *Something is building in her movements*, Nick thought, *like a storm gathering force.*

"The restaurant's just a fifteen-minute walk," Marc offered, still hovering with his wine bottle. "*On a le temps de boire un verre avant de sortir, non?*"

The suggestion hung in the air, more humid than Marc's damp blazer. Nick noticed how the hotel room had become a collection of uncomfortable territories: his mother by the window, marking her space with an empty glass; Susan perched on the sofa's arm as if ready for flight; Laslo sprawled in a chair but with tense shoulders; Marc still caught in the entryway near the door.

"God, yes, a drink," Lynne jumped at the idea. She clicked the button on the hotel phone for room service. "But Nick, you're still nursing that water. Sure you don't want something stronger?"

"The water's fine," Nick said, realizing he'd been holding the same sparkling water—when he'd wanted still—for what felt like hours. The bubbles had long since died.

"Anyway, *cinq* glasses," Lynne spoke into the phone, then added with pointed brightness, "And a corkscrew, *s'il vous plaît.*" Her forced French drew laughs, everyone's smiles breaking through at once.

Nobody knew what to say next, so they just sat there, smiles fading, as if they were all waiting for something else to be funny. Outside, the weather continued its assault on the city.

"*C'est pas possible, ce temps,*" Marc muttered, moving finally from his spot by the door to lay his wet umbrella in the bathroom. "Lynne, *ma chérie*, you should have seen the taxi driver's face when I asked to go through Saint-Germain. *Il était au bord de la crise de nerfs.*"

His casual French came off as natural and lived-in, unlike Lynne's textbook pronunciation. Nick watched his mother's face tighten almost imperceptibly at Marc's assured fluency.

"The weather was fine this morning," Susan offered.

"*Ça change vite, hein*?" Marc settled onto the sofa, forcing Susan to either sit properly beside him or move away. She chose to move, finding a new perch on the chair nearest to Lynne. "One minute you're having coffee on a terrace, the next..." He gestured to the windows.

A knock at the door made everyone start. The room service waiter entered with the corkscrew and glasses on a silver tray. The result was an obvious attempt at elegance, like everything else in the hotel desperately strove to appear.

"*Posez-le là*," Lynne instructed with careful French this time, pointing to the dresser. Nick noticed how the waiter's eyes flicked to Marc, as if seeking translation, before following Lynne's gesture.

Laslo worked the cork loose with practiced brutality, the bottle gripped between his knees. Then, circling the room, he began to offer it up.

"Not too much for me," Susan said. "We haven't eaten since breakfast."

"Except for those macarons," Lynne corrected, her voice carrying a strange edge. "From Ladurée. You insisted."

The mention of food appeared to make the room even more claustrophobic. Nick checked his phone: not quite seven-thirty. The reservation wasn't until eight-thirty, he remembered. A whole hour to fill with conversation in this overheated space.

"You must try this, Nick," Laslo insisted, pouring him a generous glass. "I had a feeling it would be exactly your taste." Nick's skin burned at the emphasis placed on "exactly." He took the glass, but the comment landed all wrong. Despite them both living in Paris, he hadn't seen Laslo in a decade—hadn't spoken to him, hadn't interacted with him.

Had Susan or his mother fed Laslo details of Nick's life? There was nothing wrong in that, he supposed. Parents talk of their children, and Susan had often said she'd wanted Nick to know he had someone nearby in Paris should he ever need anything. Still, Nick wondered how many other conversations Laslo had filed away, how many casual preferences he'd noted and stored for moments like this one, when the appearance of thoughtfulness could be weaponized into intimacy.

Come to think of it, hadn't there been moments over the years when he'd felt watched in a way he couldn't explain? He'd dismissed those feelings as paranoia, phantoms of his past making him jumpy. But now, with Laslo's eyes on him, those old sensations reemerged, took a new shape.

"Nick," Marc broke in, "tell us about this new job of yours. The one you left banking for?"

Nick sensed all eyes turn to him. Even his mother, who had been adjusting the curtains in her compulsion, turned to hear his response. The weight of their attention made the damp air stick to his skin.

"It's nothing exciting," he said, realizing the mistake even as the words left his mouth. His mother's shoulders tensed.

"Nothing exciting?" Lynne echoed, still facing the window. "Banking wasn't exciting enough for you, but now this new thing is 'nothing exciting?'"

"Well, it's different," Nick hedged, aware that every word could be a potential landmine.

"But a design studio? After all that education?"

Screw what she thinks, Nick thought. Sure, the pay was shit compared to banking, but even as a junior designer grinding out mood boards and font selections, he felt more alive than he'd ever felt moving money around spreadsheets.

"It's creative and I like that. Though the hours are still—"

"Creative!" Lynne spun from the window, her wine sloshing dangerously. "You know who was creative? Your father was creative. Always coming up with new schemes, new ideas, new—" With the abrupt stop, color rose in her cheeks.

The room went still. Even the rain let up.

"Lynne?" Susan said.

"Last I heard, he's a mechanic," Nick said. "And who cares?"

"*Was* a mechanic," Lynne said, biting her lip.

"The wine is excellent," Marc cut in, his social instincts taking over. "Laslo, you must tell me where you found this."

The room's atmosphere shifted. Nick watched his mother drain her glass and move at once to pour another. A tremor shook her hand, a slight shake he hadn't noticed before. And moreover, Nick hadn't heard her mention Gene in years. Susan watched her too, Nick noticed, with the alertness of someone who had witnessed this scene before and knew its variations.

"I think I will have something stronger," Nick said. "But gin and tonic, not wine, if there's any left."

Lynne's unblinking face, like that of a well-bred owl, brightened with dangerous enthusiasm. "Of course, my boy. Let mommy fix it for you."

"I can—" Nick started to rise.

"No, no. Let me do this for you." Her voice held an intensity that made everyone else in the room look away, finding sudden interest in their glasses, the carpet, the rain-streaked windows.

"Just a small one," Nick said, watching his mother's unsteady hands pour gin with deliberate concentration. The liquid splashed against the glass's sides.

"Remember when you first drank gin?" Lynne asked, her voice taking on that peculiar tone she used for mining the past.

"You were seventeen, at that party in Connecticut. The one at the Stevensons.'"

"No, I don't actually—" Nick began, but stopped. At seventeen, he had been living with his Aunt Julia. Lynne remembering any detail about his life then was impossible.

"Of course you do," Lynne insisted. "Susan, you remember. It was just after we'd—" She stopped again, that same abrupt halt, a record needle being lifted mid-song.

Laslo leaned forward in his chair, eyes bright with interest.

"*On devrait peut-être y aller*?" Marc suggested, checking his watch. "The rain's let up."

Susan stood first. "Yes. We should start walking if we want to make the reservation."

"My umbrella's hardly wet," Marc added. "We can share."

Nick watched his mother's face as she handed him his drink. She was searching for something he couldn't name. Grief, he thought, but when wasn't grief there? And something else slithered across her features—something coiled, waiting. He downed his drink in a swift succession of gulps.

The group spilled out of the hotel room just as the showers started again. Marc fell into step beside Nick under the inadequate shelter of the umbrella. The others forged ahead: Lynne steering Susan by the elbow, Laslo trailing behind them with histrionic complaints about his shoes.

"*Tu sais*," Marc said, low enough that only Nick could hear, "you remind me so much of your mother. The same… how do you say… *intensité*." He shifted the umbrella closer, and Nick was forced to walk smack up against his shoulder.

"I'm nothing like my mother." Nick heard how defensive he sounded. Marc's bright, knowing smile said he'd heard the edge in Nick's voice.

"No? The same beautiful eyes, at least." Marc's shoulder brushed Nick's again, not by accident this time. "The same way of holding yourself apart from everyone."

Ahead of them, Lynne's voice carried back through the downpour: "Nick! Nick, my boy, are you alright back there? You're not getting wet?"

"He's perfectly dry," Marc called back, his voice rich with amusement. "I'm taking very good care of him."

Preferring to be soaked than to endure another moment of Marc's proximity, Nick stepped sideways into the rain. He could feel the older man's eyes on him as he quickened his pace.

The water seeped through Nick's threadbare coat into his carefully chosen turtleneck, the expensive silk-cashmere blend now clinging to his shoulders in defeat. No one had even noticed his ensemble—not his mother, not Susan, not even Laslo with his artist's eye. The whole performance of the outfit, with its deliberate message of success, was now waterlogged. Water dripped from his hair onto the collar, and Nick could feel the fabric beginning to pill where his messenger bag strap crossed his chest. He'd spent nearly a month's rent on this sweater, and now the garment resembled something fished out of the Seine.

Ahead, Lynne and Susan huddled together under Laslo's umbrella, while Marc lingered behind him like an unwanted shadow. Nick felt caught between them all, soaked and invisible and somehow more exposed than if he'd shown up in rags. As they waited at the crosswalk, his mother's voice floated through, saying something about wine pairings to Susan, and Nick watched a puddle of rainwater form at his feet.

"The restaurant is just there," Marc pointed, catching up to Nick and grazing his wet shoulder. "Though perhaps we should have taken a taxi after all. You look a bit… *trempé*."

The restaurant hit them with a wall of warmth as they entered. The heat's intensity suffocated Nick under the weight of his wet clothes. A waitress took one look at their bedraggled group and hesitated before recognizing Marc, her face shifting into practiced welcome.

"*Bien sûr, la table de Monsieur Bernard*," the waitress said, and Nick noticed how his mother brightened at this evidence of Marc's local status.

They were led to a corner table—too small for five people—in a room that managed to be both grand and oppressive. Nick found himself wedged between Marc and Laslo, while his mother and Susan faced him across a forest of wine glasses and tea lights. His turtleneck steamed in the heat, and by result, gave off a damp wool smell that made him want to disappear.

"Nick should sit next to me," Lynne announced, already rising. "I can hardly see him over there."

"We've just settled," Susan murmured, but Lynne orchestrated a complicated dance of musical chairs that trapped Nick between his mother and the wall. Her perfume—Chanel No. 5, the same scent she'd worn his entire childhood—rose in waves, amplified by the rain and warmth. It coated the back of Nick's throat with syrupy sweetness. He held back a cough as something loosened in his chest: a memory of Saturday mornings at the piano, her hand on his shoulder, warm and proud. The scent disarmed him—nostalgic and cloying, a contradiction, like Lynne herself.

"There," Lynne said with satisfaction. "Now I can see everyone properly." She held the menu, unopened, like a shield. Under the table, Nick felt her knee bouncing with nervous energy. Nick remembered then when he was seventeen, sitting across from his mother in the kitchen of his Aunt Julia's home in Connecticut, an unflashy house with beige countertops and fluorescent lights.

Lynne is there on a visit. One of her infrequent and often badly timed visits. He'd been too naive then to understand why she had held that piece of paper like it might bite—the letter from his father announcing his "life changes." Gene hadn't even called it leaving. Just "changes," as if he were switching breakfast cereals or trying a new haircut.

"Your father thinks he's found himself," Lynne had said, her voice strange and wobbly in a way that scared Nick more than if she had shouted. "Right there in Missouri, can you believe it? With a woman named Kate who teaches yoga." She laughed, a sound that made Nick want to hide under the table like he used to when thunderstorms got too loud. "Yoga, my boy. Can you imagine your father doing downward dog? Right in Kansas City, ten minutes away."

Nick had sat there, watching his mother's hands shake just as they were shaking over the menu in this too-warm Paris restaurant. He remembered how the afternoon light had made patterns on the linoleum, how he'd focused on a spot of dried juice on the kitchen countertop, how time had stretched endlessly until finally Susan had arrived. Susan, who'd just been his mother's colleague at the university, someone Nick only knew as the nice lady who sometimes brought him books about France.

5.

The waiter hovered at Lynne's elbow, pen poised. Nick watched as his mother ordered for both of them in French, each syllable chiseled like crystal—precise but seconds from shattering. The foie gras to share, then duck for her, fish for him. She tilted her head toward Nick at an angle that seemed both attentive and raptorial. She hadn't asked what he wanted.

"And more wine, I think," Laslo interjected. "The same as before?" He looked at Marc, deferring to the Parisian's expertise even though Laslo had lived in the city for twenty years.

"Something lighter with the fish, perhaps," Marc suggested. He recited wine pairings like a parrot performing tricks for seed—perfect pronunciation, hollow performance. His eyes slid to Nick. "Unless you prefer red?"

Before Nick could answer, Lynne's glass clattered against a water goblet. The sound rang out, and Susan jumped. "*Pardon*," Lynne said, but she seemed to be apologizing to the table itself rather than to its occupants.

The waiter retreated, and they were left in a pocket of awkwardness. Nick became aware of other conversations flowing around them, other families and friends sharing ordinary evenings. At the next table, a child laughed. All the while, Lynne's fingers drummed absently against the table's edge, a quiet heartbeat beneath the hum of the restaurant.

"Tell me about the light studies, Laslo," Susan said with determined brightness. "You never did explain what inspired them."

"Oh, I don't want to go into that," Laslo began, already straightening in his chair. "Unless you're *really* curious. You see, I've been experimenting with the way light moves across different bodies at different intervals—"

"Will you excuse me?" Lynne interrupted, pushing back her chair. "Powder room." She stood too quickly, her white cloth napkin falling to the floor. Nick noticed how both Susan and Marc half-rose, as if anticipating the need to steady her, but Lynne had already started weaving between tables toward the back of the restaurant.

"She hasn't eaten all day," Susan said in a soft voice once Lynne had moved far enough away. The plain statement carried layers of worry beneath.

"*La pluie*," Marc offered vaguely. "It affects one's appetite."

Nick watched the space where his mother had disappeared and remembered how she used to vanish like this during his childhood suppers too—always returning with brighter eyes and slower hands.

"The foie gras is excellent here," Marc said, leaning closer to Nick again. "Though perhaps too rich for someone so… delicate." The last word carried an innuendo that made Nick grip his water glass tighter.

The starters materialized, the foie gras gleaming on its stark white plate like evidence of a small, silken secret. Nick sat trapped between the cooling food and his mother's empty chair, caught in the crossfire of competing social graces.

6.

The cold marble pressed into Lynne's palms as she gripped the edges of the sink, her fingers as pale as porcelain under the harsh bathroom light. The mirror threw back an image of wide, unblinking eyes and a face that sagged under the weight of exhaustion, her lips clenched so tight they almost disappeared. Her phone, abandoned next to the soap dispenser, displayed the text from Missouri that had carved open the morning, quietly gutting her: "Gene passed away this morning..." She reached for her lipstick like a lifeline, but her rickety fingers could not bring themselves to apply it. The expensive wallpaper, with its gilded patterns, swam mockingly in her vision.

She whispered to her reflection for strength. But even her own voice sounded foreign and ugly, filled with echoes of past bathrooms where she had sought refuge from her life. Lynne knew she needed to tell Nick about his father's passing. Telling him was the right thing to do. But every time she looked at her son tonight, wearing an expensive sweater in an attempt to impress her, she couldn't bring herself to say the words.

Another woman entered the bathroom and gave Lynne a once-over. Lynne straightened up and uncapped her lipstick, applying with a confidence and mastery that contradicted the turmoil inside her. When her phone lit up again with another message from Missouri, she ignored it. Instead, she turned the phone face down on the marble, letting the stone surface soothe her palm as tears threatened to spill from her eyes.

7.

"Have you started without me? Good, good. No sense in letting it get cold." Lynne picked up her fork but only pushed the foie gras around the porcelain plate, creating abstract patterns in the sauce. Her fingers moved with the precision of someone defusing a bomb, each stroke deliberate, as if the arrangement of the food might reveal some hidden truth.

Nick watched her hands—steadier now, but somehow worse, an artificial calm that reminded him of the way she used to arrange flowers after fights with Gene, every stem placed with habitual perfection. The conversation had drifted to Laslo's next gallery opening, his voice carrying across the table with effortless charm while Marc interrupted with elaborate suggestions that no one had asked for.

"The space has these wonderful high ceilings," Laslo gestured with his wine glass. "Perfect for large-scale installations."

"But the lighting," Marc cut in, leaning forward. "You'll need proper spotlights, of course. I know someone who did the Pompidou retrospective last spring—"

Lynne's phone rang in her purse, the sound cutting through Marc's monologue like a knife. She didn't move, her fork suspended above the plate. The phone went silent. Her shoulders relaxed a fraction. Then it rang again, the sound more insistent.

She picked up her wine glass, the stem pinched between thumb and forefinger, and then set it down without drinking. Her eyes fixed on her purse as the phone continued its insistent ringing. Nick recognized the dance; he'd seen Lynne like this before—this battle between curiosity and dread.

"Oh, for heaven's sake," she sighed, then raised her voice to a brittle brightness. "Sorry, everyone, I should check this. It might be about our flight tomorrow." She pushed back her chair, the legs scraping against the floor with a sound like a scream. Her fingers clutched her purse with the desperate strength of someone hanging from a cliff's edge.

"Lynne," Susan's voice carried a warning wrapped in softness. "Ignore it." Her hand reached across the space between them but fell short, hovering in the air like an unfinished thought.

"Just one minute, Su." Lynne's lips stretched into the same smile she'd worn at Nick's parent-teacher conferences, at church potlucks, at her younger son's funeral: a careful arrangement of muscles that never reached her eyes. She threaded her way between the tables, each step precise despite the tremble that had returned to her hands. Lynne gripped the phone, ringing again and again, like a grenade with a half-pulled pin.

Nick watched her weave through the restaurant, her back straight as a soldier's. He knew that posture too, the way she held herself when everything fell apart around her, as if good posture alone could keep the world from seeing her crack.

8.

Lynne sat in the bathroom stall farthest from the door, her hand clutching tightly to the cold metal handle. She breathed in the toilet's artificial lavender smell and tried to calm her racing mind. Her phone lit up with a new message, bringing her back to reality:

"I know this is a shock, but we need to discuss funeral arrangements. We're thinking about Thursday. Please call when you can. The girls are asking about Nick."

The girls. Gene's stepdaughters. Lynne had never met them, but she knew their names and ages from Facebook photos of Gene's second wedding. Emma and Sarah. Fifteen and twelve now. She'd watched them grow up through social media posts, through secondhand stories, through the carefully curated images Kate—Gene's second wife—shared of their perfect blended family.

Twelve. The age made Lynne's stomach clench. She remembered Nick at twelve, how he'd changed that summer. How he'd stopped playing outside, stopped having friends over. And how Jason, her younger son, had ended up the same way.

She opened Facebook and studied their photos on her phone: tacky school portraits, small-town dance recitals, cheap family vacations to campgrounds. Looking for signs she'd learned to recognize too late in her own boys. The way the girls held themselves in photos with Gene. The careful distance. The fixed smiles.

But maybe she only saw ghosts. Maybe her own guilt was painting echoes onto innocent family photos. Kate hovered in every photo, always watching. She wouldn't let… She would notice if…

Lynne put her fingers to her temples as memories flooded her mind—the morning's drama at the café where she had attacked Susan over a tip, anything to avoid saying the words: Gene is dead. She remembered how Gene had taught Nick and Jason to ride their bikes in the scorching Missouri heat. Then she remembered how Gene had missed Nick's high school graduation because one of his stepdaughters had a dance recital on the same day (and because he was just an asshole, Lynne reminded herself).

Her phone buzzed again, this time from Susan. "Are you ok?"

Lynne hovered over her keyboard, unsure of what to say. "Coming," she started typing but then deleted. "He's dead," she typed next but deleted as well. The bathroom's piped-in music played something French and jazzy, but to Lynne, the score faded into something like white noise. As she steadied herself to stand, she couldn't help but see the blue stall door as a shield between herself and the truth she would have to tell her son.

She scrolled back to the message about the girls. They were asking about Nick. Why? They'd never met him. Did they know about him, too, about Jason? Did their mother tell them anything? Or were they just curious about their stepfather's other family, the sons who never visited, who weren't in any perfect Facebook photos?

Emma looked so much like her mother in the photos. But Sarah… Sarah had that same haunted look around her eyes that Nick…

No. She couldn't think about that. Couldn't let her mind go there. She had failed her own children, but she couldn't take on the responsibility of Gene's other family too. Still, her finger hovered over the message. Should she say something? Warn someone? But warn them about what, exactly? She had no proof, no evidence, just a mother's belated instincts and a lifetime of regret.

9.

The main courses had arrived in Lynne's absence. The duck confit sat cooling on a copper platter. Nick had already eaten half his fish; he'd obviously given up waiting.

"Everything alright?" Susan asked, her fork paused midway to her mouth.

"Fine, fine," Lynne waved away the concern, but her voice held a new vacancy. "The flight's confirmed. All good." She turned to Nick with sudden intensity. "How's your fish, my boy? Is it good? It looks good. You always did love fish. Remember that place in Kansas City, by the plaza? You used to beg your father to take you there for your birthday. What was it called?"

Nick shifted in his chair. "Bristol," he said quietly. "The Bristol Seafood Grill."

"Yes! The Bristol. Your father would always order the…" She trailed off, her face gone pale. "Would anyone like more wine?"

"Lynne," Susan murmured.

"Marc, you're the expert. Should we try something else? Something special? It's a special night, after all. Our last night together."

"*Bien sûr*," Marc began, but Laslo cut him off.

"Last night together?" Laslo raised an eyebrow. "You make it sound so final, darling. No one is going anywhere. We'll all be right here in Paris next time you visit. Won't we, Nick?"

Nick nodded, pushing a piece of fish around his plate. The restaurant grew warmer, more constricting. His mother's perfume choked the air around him.

"Right here in Paris," Lynne echoed, her voice strange. "While we're in Cape Town. While life goes on. While everything…" She took a large swallow of wine. "Nick, do you remember that summer when your father tried to build a deck?"

The question came out of nowhere, and Nick's fork froze halfway to his mouth. "What?"

"The deck. Behind the house. You must have been, what, ten? Eleven? He bought all that wood, had it delivered on a Saturday morning. Said he'd finish by Sunday night."

"Lynne," Susan tried again, "perhaps we should—"

"But he didn't finish it, did he?" Lynne continued as if Susan hadn't spoken. "Just left all that lumber out there to rot. For weeks. Months. The neighbors complained. Remember?"

Nick remembered. He remembered the wood warping in the Missouri rain, his father's tools left to rust in the grass. But he said nothing, just watched his mother's hands shift and fidget among the wine glasses.

"Your father," she said, then stopped. Started again. "Your father never could finish anything he started."

Laslo and Marc exchanged glances. The waiter approached their table, sensed the tension, and retreated.

"Except dying." The words ghosted from her lips. "He managed to finish that."

The moment of silence that followed swallowed all other sounds in the restaurant—the clink of glasses, the hum of conversations, even the faint jazz from hidden speakers.

Nick's fish turned to ash in his mouth. He set his fork down with exaggerated care, aware that if he didn't focus on this simple action, something inside him might crack.

"When?" The word came out steadily, a realization which caught him off guard.

"This morning." Lynne looked down at her plate as though speaking to her uneaten duck. "At their house in Kansas City.

With her. The yoga teacher." She gave a hiccuping laugh that might have been a sob. "Heart attack. In his sleep. Very peaceful, they said. Very… neat."

Susan had gone rigid beside Lynne, her hand rooted to her glass. Even Marc and Laslo receded, as if they'd stepped back into a painting, leaving just the three of them—Nick, his mother, and Susan—in sharp focus.

"This morning," Nick repeated. The words tasted bitter. "You've known since this morning?"

"My boy—" Lynne reached for his hand across the table.

Nick pulled back, his elbow knocking against his water glass. A small splash landed on his already-ruined top. "Since this morning. Through all of… through the rain, and the wine, and—" He stopped, remembering his mother's stranger-than-usual behavior in the hotel room with sudden, sickening clarity.

"But you don't even speak to him," Lynne said, her voice edging upward. "When was the last time? Christmas? No, you didn't call this Christmas or last. His birthday? No, never. When, Nick? When did you last speak to your father? Fifteen years ago?"

The charge hung in the air like a thick smoke. Nick felt the familiar rage rise in his throat—the same rage he'd felt at twelve, at sixteen, at eighteen—but now tinged with something else.

"That's not—" he started, then stopped. Because she was right, wasn't she? When was the last time? He couldn't even picture his father's name on his phone, let alone his number. "That's not the point."

"Then what is the point?" Lynne's voice had taken on that familiar theatrical tremor. "Tell me. What is the point?"

"The point is," Nick said, each word careful and exact, "that you sat in that hotel room for hours. You watched me get soaked in the rain. You ordered dinner. You—" He hesitated. "You watched me sit here eating fish while my father was dead."

Susan moved then, her hand reaching for Lynne's shoulder. "Perhaps we should—"

"No," Lynne cut her off. "No, we shouldn't. We shouldn't… anything. Because your father, Nick, your father, he—well, I don't know what he did, to you—While I… while I…"

"Lynne, *ma chérie*," Marc leaned forward, wine sloshing in his glass, "let's not ruin a beautiful evening. Death is so… provincial."

Nick shot him a look of pure hatred, but Marc continued, oblivious or uncaring. "Besides, your son is far too gorgeous to wear such tragic expressions. It ages the face, you know."

"Marc," Susan warned, but he barreled on.

"When my father died," he announced to the table at large, his hand somehow finding its way to Nick's shoulder, "I celebrated. Ordered champagne. Danced until dawn. Much healthier than all this American melodrama, don't you think?"

"Take your hand off me," Nick said, his voice low.

Silent tears began to carve paths through Lynne's perfect makeup. "You don't understand, Nick. You never understood. Your father and his… his perfect new life. His yoga wife. His stepdaughters. While I…"

"While you what?" Nick yanked his shoulder free from Marc's grip. "While you carted me away to Julia's? Or while you used me as your emotional support animal? While you—"

"*Mon dieu*," Marc interrupted again, "the tension! It's delicious. Like a David Lynch film, but with better lighting. Nick, darling, has anyone ever told you you're absolutely radiant when you're angry?"

"For God's sake, Marc," Susan snapped, but Lynne spoke over her.

"Emotional support animal? Is that what you think?" Her voice dropped to a razor's edge. "When your father left—when he found that new family—who was there? Who held you when you cried? Who made all those trips to Connecticut to see you? Who—"

"Who used me as a weapon?" Nick's voice pitched, inching closer to hysteria. She had the history all wrong. "Who made me feel guilty every time I decided that I didn't want to see him?"

"*C'est passionnant*," Marc sighed, swirling his wine. "A Tennessee Williams play, but with better clothes. Though Nick, that *pull* really is ruined now. Such a shame. It looked so expensive."

"And it was Julia who held me," Nick added for his mother's sake.

Laslo, who had been silently watching, suddenly spoke. "I should go."

"No one is going anywhere," Lynne said, her tears vanishing in an instant. "We haven't had dessert. We're celebrating. Aren't we celebrating, Su? Our last night before South Africa?" She laughed, the sound like breaking glass. "Though I suppose now we'll have to stop in Missouri. For the funeral. Won't that be nice, Nick? A family reunion?"

"Christ!" Nick pushed back his chair. The legs screeched against the floor with a sound like a scream.

"*Attends*," Marc reached for him again. "Stay. This is so much more interesting than any usual *dîner*."

Nick jerked away from Marc's reaching hand with such violence that he knocked over his wine glass. The red liquid spread across the white tablecloth, seeping into the linen like a puncture opening.

"Don't touch me," Nick said, his voice gruff and dangerous. "Don't you dare touch me."

"Nick," Susan started. "And you," she turned to her wife, "you sat there all day. All day. Making little jokes, critiquing my clothes, my job, my life. Playing your little games over the waiter this morning. While he was dead. While your ex-husband was dead."

Lynne, ignoring Susan, turned again to Nick. "Your father, who couldn't even be bothered to call on your birthday. Or even send a text. A text! To his only son."

"Shut up," Nick said.

Lynne looked at him in surprise. Nick had never spoken to her in that tone before.

Marc, wide-eyed, leaned back in his chair and observed them like they were all characters in a play.

"I need air," Nick said, standing. His soaked turtleneck clung to him like a second skin. "I need… I just need air."

"Running away?" Lynne's voice betrayed her, guilt bleeding through the accusation. "Like father, like son?"

The words died into absolute silence. Even Marc's smirk melted away.

Nick stood frozen, one hand on his chair back, the wine still spreading across the tablecloth. The restaurant faded to silence around them, or perhaps blood just thundered in his ears.

"I'll go with you," Marc started to rise, misreading the lull in action. "*L'air fresh—*"

"No," Lynne snapped. "Sit down, Marc. For once in your life, just sit down and be quiet."

Nick's panic dissolved into a surreal serenity. He looked around at their little tableau: Laslo studying his wine glass like it held the secrets of the universe, Marc finally silenced, Susan's hand hovering near but not touching his mother's shoulder. "I can't do this anymore."

"Nick—" Lynne reached for him.

"He was my father," Nick choked out. "Whatever else he was—whatever he did or didn't do—he was my father. And you let me sit here eating and drinking while he was dead."

Then Nick did something he hadn't done in a very long time. He started to cry.

"Oh God." Lynne shot to her feet, her chair tipping back. Susan caught the edge before it fell. "Oh God, my boy."

She stepped around the table toward Nick, but he lurched back, tears still slipping down his face. He stumbled into a waiter, who stiffened and stared straight ahead, determined to ignore the scene unraveling before him.

"*C'est trop*," Marc said under his breath, but his usual dramatic tone had disappeared. He looked almost ashamed.

"Don't," Nick said to his mother. He held up his hands. "Just don't." The tears wouldn't stop, and he could feel other diners watching, could hear the muted conversations, the discrete coughs. His ruined turtleneck clung to him like a reminder of everything he'd tried to be tonight, everything he'd failed to be.

Laslo shoved his chair back. "I'll get the bill."

"Sit down," Susan said, her voice steady. "Everyone sit down. Right now." Her lecture-hall authority rang through the words, and everyone quickly dropped into their chairs. Even Nick found himself sinking back down.

"Lynne," Susan continued, "you're going to sit here and tell your son everything. About the text messages. About the arrangements or whatever. And then you're going to listen—really listen—to whatever he needs to say."

"I don't want to say anything," Nick managed. "I don't want to... I can't..."

10.

The cold hit like a slap the moment Nick stepped into the night. Smog spun with fog in lazy circles under the streetlights. He barely registered his surroundings. His breath came fast, sharp, white puffs vanishing as quickly as they appeared. His hands clenched and unclenched in the pockets of his coat. He didn't know where to go—only that he had to move.

He could still hear his mother's voice, calm, almost perfunctory, over dinner: "Heart attack. In his sleep."

That was it. No warning. No lead-up. No mention of how his mother had waited all day to tell him, as though the death of one's father were a trivial matter that could wait between the soup and the main course.

He had barely survived five minutes of conversation before shoving back his chair and walking out. Now, he stood in the Square du Vert-Galant while half-formed thoughts rattled in his head like loose change in an old jar.

Why tell him like that? And why did he even care?

The wind curled around him, cutting through his tatty, wet outerwear. A beam of bright light flashed from behind him.

"Something wrong?"

Nick turned. A uniformed police officer, arms crossed and assessing Nick, stood a few feet away.

Nick exhaled through his nose and shook his head. Had he been talking to himself? Wouldn't be the first time.

"*Vous allez bien?*"

"*Oui, monsieur, juste—*" Nick hesitated, searching for something that wouldn't sound insane. "Just trying to collect my thoughts."

The policeman gave him a look, noticed how close Nick sat near the edge of the riverbank, and then switched to broken English. "You are not thinking of doing anything stupid?"

Nick huffed out something like a laugh. "*Mais non!*"

"You are drinking?"

"Not enough."

The officer smirked. "*Alors, bonne nuit.*"

Nick nodded. "And to you, *monsieur*—?" Why ask this man his name? One didn't do that—ask strangers their names. But Nick felt desperate for a connection just then.

"Hertzberg."

Nick's mouth worked before his brain caught up. "Hertzberg, like Leo Hertzberg from *What I Loved*?"

The cop squinted. "What is that?"

"Oh, just a book. My favorite book."

Nick stared at the dark water. Somewhere beneath that oily surface, the city's history flowed past, centuries of secrets drifting toward the sea. He'd read once that some archaeologists had found ancient boats preserved in the river mud, their wood still intact after hundreds of years. Time moves differently down in the dark, where memories go to die.

He could still hear his mother's voice, that carefully modulated tone she reserved for grave moments: "He managed to finish that." As if death were just another task Gene had completed, like fixing a car or building a deck or destroying his sons.

Officer Hertzberg evidently had nowhere to be. He stooped down and sat next to Nick along the riverbank. "*Alors,* what's wrong with you? Girl troubles?"

Nick gave a bitter laugh. "No, nothing like that." The words formed in his mouth like a language he'd only half-learned. *I should be… something*, he thought. Sad maybe. Or angry. But here he sat, talking to a cop in the cold.

"*Mon père, il est mort. Aujourd'hui.*"

The truth sat there between them, not moving, not changing.

"*Je suis désolé*," Officer Hertzberg said, his head down.

Then the words tumbled out of Nick before he could stop them. "Soon, I won't even remember if he was ever alive. And if someone who looks like him brushes past me on some crowded sidewalk, my heart won't jolt. Not the way it used to when I was a kid, when I thought I heard his voice in another room. And that's good, I guess. Really good, actually."

Hertzberg shifted his weight, eyeing Nick. "I don't really understand."

Nick huffed another dry laugh. "Yeah, neither do I."

Silence hung between them. Cutting through the square, a wind rattled the skeletal branches overhead.

Hertzberg cleared his throat. "*Donc*, what are you going to do?"

Nick glanced at the police officer. This man wasn't filling silence. He was taking a reading—watching for Nick's next move.

Nick turned away, staring at the frozen ground. "I don't know."

A shuffling noise drew their attention. Through the fog, a figure huddled against one of Pont Neuf's stone pillars—an elderly woman with a cardboard sign propped against her knees. She didn't look up or reach out, just kept her eyes fixed on some middle distance, lips moving in silent prayer or conversation with herself.

Nick paused. The woman's stillness carried the weight of an accusation.

"*Une autre stupide SDF*," Officer Hertzberg warned.

But Nick walked over to the woman and crouched beside

her. Up close, he could see her face mapped with deep lines, skin roughened like old leather. Her eyes, when they finally met his, were startlingly clear.

"*Vous avez faim?*"

Before she could answer, Hertzberg stepped between them. "There are shelters for people like this. Places they can go."

"Places that are full," Nick said. "Or unsafe." Words from long ago, buried and submerged, now lifted to the surface. "There but for the grace of God," Gene had once said, the only kind thing Nick had ever heard his father say.

The woman still hadn't spoken, but her hands were working something in her lap: a small piece of bone-white string, knotted and unknotted with practiced movements.

Nick reached into his pocket and pulled out some coins. He placed them beside her without ceremony.

She looked at the offering, then back at Nick. Her fingers stilled on the string. "*Merci*," she breathed, then added something else—a blessing maybe, or a curse—in a language Nick didn't recognize.

Hertzberg made a disgusted sound and walked away, but Nick knelt there a moment longer, watching as the woman pocketed the coins into the recesses of her clothing.

"I'm sorry," Nick said, though he wasn't sure what he was apologizing for—her circumstances, his privilege, or the general unfairness of the world.

Nick watched the officer disappear into the fog, his flashlight's beam creating a halo that grew fainter with each step. He wondered if Gene had ever given money to strangers, if he'd ever felt that basic human connection to someone else's suffering. Probably not. Gene's world had been too ordered, too controlled for such spontaneous acts of kindness.

The wind picked up, carrying the smell of wet stone and diesel exhaust. Nick pulled his collar higher, though the cold had settled somewhere deeper than his skin. His clothes, still damp from the rain, clung to him, and each of his steps was accompanied by the soft squelch of wet leather on concrete. The sound echoed of summers in Missouri, of running through sprinklers in the backyard, of the way water could be both play and punishment depending on whose hands controlled it.

Nick watched the streetlights glow against the spreading fog. He could almost imagine stepping back in time, rewinding the night:

He could have stayed at dinner. Kept his mouth shut. Asked his mother questions instead of shutting down. He could have listened. Maybe even cried some more. Perhaps left the table feeling less like a frayed thread of something once whole.

But going back was no longer an option.

Walking away from Square du Vert-Galant, he only glanced back once. He could come back tomorrow, sit on a bench, and listen to the silence of the stars. For now, he just kept walking.

His apartment waited somewhere in the maze of streets ahead, its single light burning like a question mark against the night. He let his feet carry him through neighborhoods he barely recognized. Past shuttered cafés where chairs stood stacked like skeletal sentries. Past graffitied walls where spray-painted faces watched with vacant eyes. Past windows where other people's lives played out in tableaus of family dinners and evening routines.

Each step put more distance between him and that restaurant, between the person he'd been before his mother's words and whoever he would become now. The city absorbed him, anonymous and indifferent, its ancient stones holding centuries of other people's grief. Somewhere behind him, his mother and Susan would be leaving the restaurant, hailing a taxi, and returning to their hotel to pack for a funeral.

11.

Nick sat in his shadowy apartment in his wet clothes, staring at the single light he'd left on earlier. Had it been hours or years since he'd stood here, dreaming of returning home after dinner? The light might as well have belonged to someone else, some other Nick who hadn't yet learned that his estranged father was dead.

His wet clothes seeped into the cushion of his gray linen sofa. He could feel the water spreading, darkening the fabric, probably ruining it. Hours ago, in what felt like another life, he would have leapt up, grabbed towels and chemical stain removers—he'd saved for six months to afford that sofa—but now, lethargy weighed too heavy for him to move. The rain had started again, harder now, drumming against the windows with perfunctory persistence. Each drop pulled at his memory, dragging him back to another rainy day, another moment when things had shifted.

He'd been thirteen, sitting on his bed in Missouri, listening to his parents argue downstairs. Not the usual kind of argument—not about bills or school or whose turn it was to do what—but something different, something too obscene to be spoken of. His father's voice rose up through the floor: "I can't keep pretending." Then his mother's: "Pretending what? That you love them?" A door slammed. Then another. Nick had sat there for hours, waiting for someone to come up and explain, to tell him what to do next. But no one had come, and in the end, the fight was just one of many that threatened to leave them with a "broken home," that ugly phrase people shirked from.

A sharp buzz cut through the memory. Nick started, realizing he'd been sitting in the near-dark for the better part of an hour. The doorbell buzzed again.

For one wild moment, Nick thought his father had come, ready to explain everything at last. Then he remembered, the knowledge hitting him fresh. His father would never explain anything again.

The buzzer sounded a third time, more insistent.

Through the intercom, Laslo's voice crackled: "Nick? I know you're up there. I can see your light." A pause. "I'm worried about you. We all are."

Nick pressed his forehead against the cool wall beside the intercom. "I'm fine."

"Darling, you're many things, but fine isn't one of them. Let me up. I brought wine."

Nick buzzed him in without answering, then listened to Laslo's leaden footsteps echoing up the stairwell. Each step matched the pounding in his head. When Laslo knocked, Nick opened the door without turning on any more lights.

"Oh, sweetheart," Laslo said, taking in Nick's soaked clothes and tear-streaked face. "You look absolutely dreadful." He swept past Nick into the apartment, balancing two bottles of wine and a bag of frozen peas. For a moment, Nick tried to see the apartment through Laslo's eyes. What would he make of the obsessively curated bookshelf with its rows of spines lined up by color and height, a weekend's work disguised as effortless style? It was the kind of detail meant to earn compliments like "so put-together," the kind Nick would accept with a modest smile, never admitting how much he'd labored over it. But now, with someone actually here, he couldn't help but wonder: Did Laslo see the polish or the need beneath it?

"Your mother sent me. Well, not exactly. She thinks I'm still at the restaurant, smoothing things over with the *maître d*." He set the wine down and held up the peas as if in explanation.

"Susan knows I'm here. Marc wanted to come himself, but we all agreed that would be—" He fluttered a hand in the air, letting the thought finish itself.

"A disaster?" Nick said, his voice rough.

"I was going to say 'inappropriate,' but yes, disaster works too." Laslo set everything down on Nick's coffee table. "Now, are you going to change out of those wet clothes, or shall I stand here and catch pneumonia just looking at you?"

"I don't have anything clean," Nick lied, but his feet carried him to his bedroom anyway. Halfway there, he caught himself—Laslo was still a stranger, standing in his apartment like it was normal. The thought scraped against something instinctive, but Nick didn't stop. He left Laslo to rummage through the cupboards. From the other room, Nick could hear glass clinking, drawers opening and closing, then Laslo's amused voice: "Good God, darling, do you alphabetize your spices? Anise to za'atar?" A pause, more clinking. "And matching wine glasses, all facing the same direction. It's like a *Le Bon Marché* catalog in here." Another drawer. "Have you ever actually cooked anything, or would that disturb the exhibition?"

Nick peeled off the ruined turtleneck. The silk-cashmere blend had dried stiff and wrong. He let it fall to the floor, a dark puddle of failure. The rest of his clothes followed: the carefully chosen black jeans, the expensive socks, all parts of a costume for a performance that had gone terribly wrong.

"Do you need help in there?" Laslo called out.

"I'm fine," Nick answered, pulling on old sweatpants and a faded T-shirt from some college event he couldn't remember. When he returned to the living room, Laslo had already uncorked the wine and held the bag of frozen peas in one hand. Nick paused. Something about it—the quiet domesticity, or the casualness with which Laslo moved through his space—unsettled him.

"For your eyes," Laslo said. "They're quite swollen. Crying doesn't suit your bone structure." He handed Nick a very full glass of red wine. "Though I must say, vulnerability becomes you in other ways."

Nick took the wine but ignored the peas. "Why are you really here, Laslo? You're sounding like that idiot Marc."

Laslo settled onto the couch, his usual posture somehow more natural, perhaps even careless, in the dim light. "Because someone needed to be. And because…" He took a long sip of wine. "Because I knew your father too, you know. Years ago, before the yoga teacher, before your parents split. Back then, he was just Gene, Lynne's country-hick-of-a-husband who always asked about my work like he actually cared." Laslo set his wine glass directly on the glass coffee table—no coaster—the red wine glowing like a warning light against the pristine surface. "Your father, he had a way of making everyone feel… something. Even me, this pretentious young artist who'd latched onto his wife's academic circle. He'd ask these questions about painting and composition that seemed so genuine, mostly because he was so clueless. He was somehow naive, I suppose you'd say. But then…"

Nick sank deeper into the sofa, the wine already warming his cold limbs. "But then?"

"But then I'd watch him with your mother. How he'd look right through her, even though everyone—everyone—could see what was happening with her and Susan. The way they orbited each other in department meetings, at faculty parties. The electricity between them." Laslo's voice had gone soft. "Your father acted like he couldn't see it. Or wouldn't. As if acknowledging their connection would mean acknowledging his own…" He trailed off.

"His own what?"

"Irrelevance, I suppose." Laslo moved closer, his knee brushing Nick's, his arm sprawling across the back of the sofa. The apartment's careful geometry began to bend around Laslo's presence—wine glasses leaving rings on the table, cushions compressed and askew, the controlled space suddenly feeling like a museum Nick had been living in rather than a home. "Gene would use your mother's sexuality as an excuse, you know," Laslo went on. "'She's leaving me for a woman,' he'd tell people, as if that made his running off with another woman somehow noble. As if he hadn't already checked out years before."

Laslo had moved closer, leg against leg. Nick noticed but didn't move. The wine flowed through him, along with exhaustion and grief. Outside, the rain still thudded on the windows. Through the multitude of other thoughts swirling in his head, Nick wondered how Laslo knew so much about Gene. From what Nick remembered, Laslo had only lived in Missouri for a short time—but then again, he was clearly a gossip, wasn't he?

"More wine?" Laslo reached for the bottle, his body turning toward Nick's in a way both casual and deliberate. Their fingers brushed as Nick surrendered his glass.

"Everything's always so charged with your mother," Laslo continued, his voice dropping lower as he topped up Nick's glass. "Everything's always life or death, passion or betrayal. But your father… he was all absences. Empty spaces where feelings should be."

Laslo's words settled in Nick's chest alongside the wine's warmth, and Nick became certain of something else, of Laslo's reason for coming, a truth as dizzying and heady as cabernet. Laslo's shoulder butted against his, solid and present, anchoring him to this moment when everything else felt adrift.

"I watched you tonight," Laslo said. "In that beautiful sweater, trying so hard to be seen. Not by your mother—she sees everything, feels everything, too much really. But trying to be seen... properly. As yourself."

"I see you," he added, even softer, turning to face Nick fully now. His hand found Nick's knee, his touch like an electric current. Laslo's dishevelment, his careless occupation of the space, felt like someone had finally opened a window in a room Nick hadn't realized was airless.

"I've always seen you," Laslo said.

Nick knew he should move away. Should say something about grief and vulnerability and bad decisions. Instead, he found himself giving in to Laslo's touch without resistance, even as every synapse in his brain screamed "run away."

"This is a terrible idea," the words left Nick's mouth just as Laslo's hand found his chest, feeling the heartbeat beneath cheap, scratchy fabric.

"The worst," Laslo agreed, and kissed him.

Nick had imagined this kiss—he saw that now, the truth emerging from some hidden corner of his mind. A pubescent boy, who lusted over his mother's friend, who lusted over any being that hadn't been Gene. But Laslo's lips moved against his with a gentle insistence that surpassed every fantasy, tasting of wine and the ghost of cigarettes. Nick responded with a desperation that shocked him, his hands clutching at Laslo's shirt.

"Wait," Nick pulled back, the room spinning. "Susan and my mother—you *know* them."

"Ancient history," Laslo purred against his neck. "A different lifetime." His hands were in Nick's hair now, gentle but sure. "Before you grew up to be so beautiful."

Nick should have found the comment creepy, should have been repelled by the whole situation—his father dead less than twenty-four hours, his stepmother's friend pushing him into the sofa cushions. Instead, a wild sort of freedom coursed through him. As if by doing this one outrageous thing, he could somehow erase the perfect son he'd tried to be, the dutiful son who had been caught in his parents' gravitational pull.

"We shouldn't," Nick said again, but his hands were already working at Laslo's shirt buttons.

"No," Laslo agreed, helping him with the buttons. "Shouldn't we?" He pulled back, studying Nick's face in the dim light. "Tell me to stop, and I will."

Nick answered by kissing him harder. Drowning felt better than breathing. Laslo's hands slid under Nick's shirt, hot against his ribs, warm against his chilled skin.

12.

Taking a cigarette out of the pack in Laslo's trousers, Nick sat smoking at his window in nothing but his sweatpants. Behind him, Laslo napped on the couch, one arm thrown across his face. They hadn't made it to the bedroom. Maybe they hadn't wanted to, as if crossing that threshold would have made everything too real.

Nick's phone buzzed on the windowsill: Susan. "Are you safe?" Then, a moment later: "Your mother finally fell asleep. The hotel doctor gave us sleeping pills."

Nick took a long drag of the cigarette. The ash threatened to fall on the windowsill—he'd never smoked in here before, another rule broken. His father used to secretly smoke in their backyard in Missouri, always carrying breath mints to divert Lynne. Another thing Nick hadn't thought about in years. The memories were starting to surface now, floating up through dark water.

He typed back: "I'm home. I'm fine."

Susan: "Try to sleep, Nick. Tomorrow will be harder."

He stubbed out the cigarette and looked back at Laslo's sleeping form. In the strange hour between night and morning, what they'd done felt both meaningless and huge, like a dream that follows you into waking.

His father was dead. The thought stung anew, sharp as glass.

Behind him, Laslo stirred. "Come back to bed." He caught himself. "Come back to the couch." His voice held a note of amusement that made Nick's skin crawl.

"You should go," Nick said, still staring out the window. The streets were empty now, glossy with rain.

"Darling—"

"Don't call me that." Nick's voice hardened. "Please just… don't."

Laslo sat up, his hair mussed in an artful way even now. "You're not going to do the gay panic thing, are you? It's so beneath you."

"This isn't about that. My father is dead."

"Yes," Laslo said, all artifice dropping from his voice. "He is."

Laslo's movements were careful, as though he were trying not to startle a wild animal. He began gathering his clothes from where they'd been scattered across the floor—his shirt draped over the armchair, his belt curled near the geometric rug that Nick waited for three months to go on sale.

Nick's phone buzzed again. His mother this time: "I need you."

His fingers moved in rapid succession: "Aren't you sleeping?" He hovered on send, then flicked the phone off. More lies.

Lynne again: "I'm sorry."

Then: "Please."

"Lynne?" Laslo asked, buttoning his shirt.

Nick nodded.

"She'll want to talk about the funeral," Laslo said. "About Missouri. About everything."

"I know."

Nick turned from the window. Fully dressed but rumpled, Laslo's bohemian appearance had been restored, yet the grey of late night revealed something older, more vulnerable in his features.

"This can't happen again," Nick said, his voice hoarse.

Laslo nodded, a sad smile playing at the corners of his mouth. "Of course not. It was a moment of… let's call it shared grief."

"It wasn't grief," Nick said sharply. "It was…"

"A mistake?" Laslo offered.

"No. Yes. I don't know." Frustrated, Nick ran a hand through his hair. "It was something else. Something I can't name."

Laslo moved closer, but stopped short of touching Nick. "It doesn't have to be anything, you know. It can just be what it was: a night, a connection. Nothing more."

Nick's jaw clenched, but he forced a smile and shrugged. "It's nothing," he lied. He didn't want Laslo to see the emotions churning inside him: anger, confusion, hurt. "Just go," he said through gritted teeth, turning away before Laslo could see the tears pooling in his eyes.

Two

1.

Nick woke to sunlight cutting across his face, his body curled tight against the pillows. Everything in his room had been carefully curated to evoke a sense of calm: gray and white bedding like cumulus clouds, walls the color of morning fog over the Seine, and yet the memory of hands on his skin made him shudder. Not just Laslo's touches from last night, but all the accumulated touches of his life, wanted and unwanted, given and taken.

He sat up too quickly, head spinning. His phone had died sometime in the night, the screen black and accusatory. Lynne's last messages gone unanswered. In the morning light, his apartment looked like a crime scene: wine glasses on the coffee table, his ruined sweater still crumpled, a strange sock that must be Laslo's lying under the window incriminatingly.

In the shower, Nick turned the water as hot as he could bear. He scrubbed his skin until it hurt, watched the soap swirl down the drain. What had he been thinking? Laslo, of all people. Laslo, who'd known him as a child. Laslo, who'd seen Nick hiding under tables with books while the adults got drunk and argued about French literature at department parties.

The water couldn't wash away the memory of how easily he'd given in, how desperately he'd sought that contact. As if physical touch could somehow fill the void his father's death and mother's secrets had torn open. As if anything could fill that emptiness.

His phone, plugged in by the bed, began to buzz with incoming messages. Nick stood dripping on the bathroom tile, unable to move, unable to face whatever his mother needed him to be today.

The buzzing continued, relentless. Nick wrapped a towel around his waist and watched his phone vibrate across the bedside table like something alive.

Finally, he picked it up: six missed calls from his mother, two from Susan, and a text from Laslo that made his stomach lurch: "Last night was lovely, darling. Let's not make it complicated."

The word "darling" slithered up Nick's skin. He deleted the message, then deleted it from the "recently deleted" folder too, as if erasing all evidence could really undo what had happened. His wet hair, dripping onto the phone's screen, blurred the remaining notifications.

More messages from his mother appeared: "Nick, we need to discuss arrangements," "The funeral is Thursday," "Should we change our flights?" "Please call me," "Nick?" "Please."

He set the phone down and peered into his floor-length mirror. The reflection showed him someone he didn't quite recognize: pale, eyes red-rimmed, a small bruise on his neck that made him want to button his collar higher. Nick cataloged the remnants of last night on his body like a crime scene investigator. An aubergine-tinted bruise on his collarbone. Violet scratches on his back, sensitive beneath his grazing shirt. Each mark served as a reminder that he had let someone—Laslo, of all people—map his body with desperate hands. But the marks were proof of something far worse: He had surrendered control to another man. That was a promise he had sworn never to break again.

And worse still, for one reckless moment, he'd convinced himself he'd wanted it. That he'd reached for Laslo just as hungrily, let himself believe in the illusion of need rather than the truth of his own weakness.

Running his fingers over the bruise on his neck, he remembered those teenage years after fumbling encounters, how shame had followed the proof of desire, each mark a secret he'd hidden beneath careful layers of clothing and lies. This moment felt no different. Last night violated something—his body and some boundary he hadn't known he needed to protect, a line crossed that he could never uncross. Laslo had known him as a child—had sung at one of his birthday parties, for Christ's sake—had lounged in his parents' backyard sipping wine while Nick hunched over homework at the kitchen table. All the while, Nick had stolen glances at this sophisticated friend of his mother's, a man who inhabited a world so different from their suburban existence. He had never imagined that more than a decade later, those worlds would collide with such force.

He turned away from the mirror, but not before catching sight of another mark just above his hip. He began to dress with methodical detachment: underwear, socks, jeans, a plain black hoodie. No expensive sweaters today. No performances. The simple act of covering his body became monumental, each layer of clothing clad him in an armor to counter the world.

His phone lit again on the nightstand—his mother, probably, or worse, Laslo—but he couldn't bring himself to look at it. Instead, he found himself opening his laptop, typing his father's name into Google. There it appeared: An obituary in the *Kansas City Star*. Gene Harrison, 54, beloved husband, stepfather, "community member." No mention of a son.

Nick slammed the laptop shut, but not before the words "beloved stepfather" burned themselves into his mind. His hands clenched as he fought to steady his breath. The room closed around him, suffocating him under the weight of memories he had spent years pretending didn't exist—his father's workshop in the backyard, the worn leather chair salvaged from some forgotten dump, the quiet click of the door locking. And later, the way his father would ruffle his hair at dinner, casual, effortless, as if nothing had happened.

And now, Laslo's touch had dragged it all back to the surface. The way Nick had frozen when Laslo's fingers brushed his hair. The way something inside Nick had splintered, even as he had pulled Laslo closer, desperate to prove… what? That this time, he could take control? That this time, he could choose?

His phone buzzed again. Susan this time: "Your mother's asking for you. But if you need space…"

Space. Nick almost laughed. What he needed was a new body, one without memory, one that didn't flinch at unexpected touches, one that didn't carry maps of old wounds beneath its skin.

He caught his reflection again in the mirror and quickly turned away. The bruise on his neck throbbed in time with his heartbeat. His father was dead, but the locks were still turning, the doors still closing.

"Fuck," Nick said to the empty room. Then louder: "FUCK." The sound echoed off the bedroom's bare walls. He grabbed his phone, needing to silence its constant buzzing, and hurled it onto the mattress. His phone bounced once and fell to the floor.

Another memory surfaced: being sixteen, throwing his phone across his bedroom at his aunt's house. His mother had called to say she wouldn't be coming to see him that weekend. Again. "It might be better for everyone if we had some distance," she'd said.

Distance. She'd given him distance, alright. Everyone in his life had been good at distance. In fact, he'd gotten so good at distance that even last night, with Laslo's hands on him, he'd felt miles away from his own body.

His mother's voice floated up again: "Why don't you ever let me hug you properly?" He'd been fourteen then, flinching away from her touch. He couldn't tell her why. Couldn't explain how every touch had become a threat, how his skin had become a border he had to defend. No wonder he'd been so quick to embrace her last night, if only to prove to himself that he could.

Now here he was, in his twenties, standing in his Paris apartment, examining marks on his body left by a man who'd known him since childhood. A man who'd been there, who might have seen something, who might have known…

Nick rested his forehead against the cold window. Below, Paris stirred to life, bakers and street cleaners beginning their morning routines, oblivious to how Nick's world had shattered twice in twenty-four hours. And now, unbidden, Laslo's touch summoned another memory, something similarly painful, something Nick hadn't thought of in years—that day at school when the police had come. He'd been in French class, conjugating verbs, when they'd called him to the principal's office.

He'd known, somehow, even before they started asking questions. Known from the way his younger brother Jason had stopped speaking to him at home, had started sleeping on the sofa instead of in the bedroom they'd shared their whole lives. Known from the whispers at church, the way the youth pastor's eyes had slid past him.

Inside the principal's office, Nick had been greeted not by the familiar face of their school administrator, but by two stern police detectives. A wave of apprehension swept over him as he stepped inside, the office small and claustrophobic.

"Have a seat," one of the detectives gestured, his voice level but unyielding.

Nick obliged, placing himself in the chair opposite them, the barrier of the desk between them.

"Your brother has made some serious allegations against you," the first detective had said.

Nick stared ahead, counted the coffee stains on the principal's desk. One, two, three. The world slowed as he nodded, everything taking on crystalline clarity.

"Several members from your church have come forward with concerns." The detective paused, glancing at his partner before looking back at Nick. "They claim you've been involved in inappropriate behavior with your younger brother."

The words struck Nick like a physical blow. The room blurred as he struggled to process the accusation—an unexpected turn, a sharp rupture that threatened to upend his already chaotic world.

"What kind of behavior?" Nick managed to stutter out, his mind spinning. The mention of his brother felt surreal, a sickening dream.

"We are referring to allegations of a sexual nature," the first detective replied, fixing Nick with a blunt gaze.

Their questions had been careful, clinical. Words like "inappropriate touching" and "incidents" floating in poisonous air. Nick had watched his hands in his lap, thinking how small they looked, how young he still was. Fifteen. Just fifteen. And Jason, just three years younger. The same age Nick had been when it had started with Gene.

The second detective, who until now had been silent, finally spoke. "These accusations, they stem directly from your brother," he said. "Jason? That's his name, right? Well, he confided in the youth pastor at your church, who then felt obliged to report the allegations to the police."

There he paused, a moment for his words to sink in, before he continued. "We've been told that you invited your brother into your bedroom on several occasions and performed inappropriate acts."

Each word was a blow to the gut. The allegations weren't just false—they were ridiculous to anyone who understood Nick's reality. With Gene's constant presence and Lynne's ever-watchful eye, he could rarely be alone, let alone be in a position to do what they were suggesting. And yet, for all its absurdity, the weight of the claim crushed his soul.

Looking back at that conversation, with the clarity of hindsight, there were elements of the situation that were undeniably wrong. There should have been a representative with him, a parent, a teacher, or even a school administrator—someone to provide support. A child should never have been left alone to navigate an interrogation by police detectives. But as a child, Nick hadn't thought of these things. He had been swallowed by fear, anxiety, and confusion. He had simply managed the best he could, even when the situation seemed beyond his ability to cope with.

That night, his mother hadn't looked at him during dinner. Jason had eaten in their bedroom. The silence had stretched between them until finally, she'd said, "I've called your Aunt Julia."

Within a week, he'd moved to his aunt's house in Connecticut, enrolled in a new school where nobody knew him or Jason or anything about the allegations that had disappeared as quickly as they'd emerged. His mother's only explanation: "Some distance might be good for everyone right now."

Distance. As if moving him across the country could erase what the detectives had said. As if geographical space could heal whatever had broken in their family. His aunt had never asked about his sudden arrival, had simply enrolled him in school and found him a therapist who asked careful questions about his childhood that Nick had never found a way to answer.

Now, standing in his Paris apartment with Laslo's marks still fresh on his skin—marks which were not painful, but shameful—Nick reconsidered Jason's accusations. Back then, the allegation had seemed like just another act of cruelty from a brother whose specialty was cruelty. Jason, the same brother who'd killed Nick's hamster and told him it had run away, who'd shown Nick's private journal to the entire youth group, who'd smiled that mean little smile every time he made Nick cry. Jason had been the true definition of a mean-spirited bully, but also just a "troubled" kid, desperate for attention.

But now, with his father dead, all those locked doors in his mind kept swinging open. Through accusing Nick, had Jason really been accusing Gene? Gene had stopped talking to Jason after Jason started at Bible college in Missouri, at least according to Lynne. Why had his father stopped all communication? Nick wondered. And then, two months into his freshman year—barely time for the leaves to turn on campus—Jason had been found hanging from his dorm room ceiling. Depression, they'd said. Just depression.

Nick had been in Paris by then and had learned the news through a terse email from his mother, not even a phone call. But then he hadn't felt anything really, except perhaps a distant relief that Jason couldn't hurt him anymore. But now... the pieces were assembling themselves with terrible lucidity. Jason's sudden claim against Nick. Gene's withdrawal from both sons. The silence that followed. And then the rope in that dorm room. "Oh God," Nick said to his reflection. His legs gave out, and he sank to the floor, the cold tiles seeping through his clothes against his skin. Nick could remember Jason's face the last time he'd seen him, at church the Sunday before Nick left for Julia's. That mean smile had slipped for just a moment, and something else had shown through—something desperate and pleading that Nick had been too angry to recognize. Had Jason been trying to tell him something? Had he been crying out for help in the only way he knew how?

The morning light crept through the window too bright, too exposing. Nick covered his eyes with his palms until he saw stars, as if he could push these realizations back into whatever dark corner they'd emerged from.

Nick gathered himself and lurched toward the kitchen. His trembling hands betrayed him, and coffee grounds scattered across the worktop. Each movement echoed from somewhere far away, untethered from his body, and Nick watched himself perform these mundane tasks from a great distance.

That last Sunday at church—the memory was sharper now. Jason, standing by the fellowship hall door, had been picking at a loose thread on his shirt sleeve. Nick had walked past him without a word, too hurt, too angry to even look at him. But now he remembered the way Jason had reached out, had almost grabbed Nick's sleeve, then let his hand fall back.

The coffee machine gurgled to life. Nick leaned against the cabinet, sifting through fragments he hadn't let himself piece together before—how Jason had started wearing long sleeves even in summer. How he'd stopped showering after gym class. How Jason had begged not to go to Bible college, but Gene had insisted. "It'll straighten you out," Gene had said. But could Nick trust his mother's recounting of what happened? Their family spoke in layers of filtered truth, each story wrapped in someone else's until reality blurred like coffee grounds in water. By September, Jason had gone—first to college, then forever. Another bracketed absence in their history, another silence they'd learned not to name.

Nick, continuing to ignore his phone, pictured his mother in her hotel room, probably still in last night's clothes, Susan hovering nearby with concern. They'd be leaving for South Africa soon. The funeral would delay them, but they'd still go. Life would go on.

But Jason's life hadn't gone on. And now Gene had gone too, taking whatever truth he knew to his grave.

Nick stared at his untouched coffee, and a strange resolve began to form. Marc would know. Marc had been there through Gene's departure, the allegations, Jason's death. Marc, who collected everyone's secrets like precious relics, who observed everything with those cool Parisian eyes.

Nick's skin crawled at the thought of seeing Marc again after last night's inappropriate flirtations, but he had more important matters to handle. Marc lived in that old building near Saint-Sulpice. He'd be home now, nursing a hangover probably, organizing his day around caffeine and complaints.

Ignoring the cascade of notifications from his mother, Nick grabbed his phone and found Marc's contact. His thumb hovered over the number. Marc had always made those little comments that rode the line between avuncular and inappropriate. But Marc had also been there at the faculty parties, had seen Gene in unguarded moments, had witnessed the slow dissolution of their family from his privileged position as Lynne's confidant.

Before he could talk himself out of it, Nick hit the call

button. The phone rang three times before Marc's voice, rough with sleep or wine or both, answered.

"*Mon Dieu*, Nick. It's not even noon."

"I need to talk to you," Nick said. "About Gene. About Jason."

A long pause stretched between them. The flirtation drained from Marc's voice. "Come over. Now."

2.

The stale, musty air in the apartment hung trapped. A doormat-sized entryway branched into a cramped, greasy kitchen on the right and a dining nook on the left, a corner barely large enough for a card table. A wall divided this area from the living-cum-sleeping room, where four barred windows overlooked a litter-strewn street to the south. Any view of the beautiful Saint-Sulpice church was completely obstructed. The long, narrow room contained a wooden bed frame shoved against one wall and, in the opposite corner, an abandoned futon. Marc moved through the cramped space with practiced grace, like a caged songbird who'd long ago memorized every perch, every limit of his confinement.

"The futon is almost never used," Marc said, launching into a convoluted story. When he moved in decades ago, the previous tenant had left it behind, but Marc hadn't touched it because he'd moved in with his sort-of boyfriend, Clément. Not really a boyfriend, more like a "*un super copain de baise*" as Marc put it, immediately cringing at his own words. "God, I was such an *imbécile* back then," he added with a laugh.

Nick hadn't imagined Marc living in such a space—definitely not chic, and not even shabby chic.

"What do you think, Nick?" Marc asked.

Nick eyed the squalor and felt a flash of recognition—his own place hadn't been much to look at either, not when he'd first rented it. But at least he'd chosen to do something about it and worked hard to shape it into something livable. Not perfect, maybe, but clean and cared for. Maybe even *raffiné,* on good days. Marc appeared to no longer care at all.

"I think it's perfect," Nick said instead. Marc screeched with delight.

"Tea?" Marc moved toward the kitchen, his usual flair replaced by an unfamiliar tentativeness. "Or coffee? Though I warn you, it's terrible coffee. You know, Nespresso capsules."

Nick remained in the cramped room and took in the disappointing reality of Marc's life. A stack of old Le Monde newspapers teetered on a coffee table, and a single Matisse print hung crookedly on the wall, the kind you could buy at any *bouquiniste*. The morning light filtered through the barred windows, etching patterns across the floor.

"Coffee's fine," Nick said, though he had no intention of drinking anything. His insides twisted from the revelations of the morning and from the drive across Paris in a taxi he couldn't afford. The seats had smelled of stale cigarettes, the scent rubbing raw against his nerves.

"Sit, sit," Marc gestured toward a worn armchair. "Though perhaps not there; the springs are murderous." He disappeared into the kitchen, where Nick could hear him banging cupboards and muttering in French.

Nick chose the edge of the futon instead, his back straight, hands clasped in his lap. How many times had Marc sat in this shabby apartment, listening to Lynne's stories over the phone about her sons? What had he known about Gene, about Jason, about any of their stories?

"So," Marc emerged with two chipped mugs. "You want to talk about your brother."

"About Jason. And Gene." Nick took the offered mug but didn't drink. "You were there, weren't you? When it all happened?"

Marc settled into the murderous armchair after all, crossing his legs with less grace than usual. His theatrical mannerisms from last night were replaced by something more genuine and therefore less unsettling.

"I was there," Marc said with care. "For some of it. Your mother… she was very broken by it all. The accusations, then later, the suicide." He paused. "Though we never called it that, did we?"

"Depression," Nick said. "That's what everyone said. Just depression."

"Ah." Marc studied his coffee. "But you're thinking now it wasn't just depression."

Shadows like slowly descending prison bars crept across the floor to touch Nick's feet. Coffee aroma mingled with the musty scent of loneliness that had seeped into the walls like a slow-acting poison, accumulating over the years. Loneliness had become part of the very structure of the place, infiltrating every crack and crevice, demanding notice. Nick knew that feeling.

"Gene used to call me into his workshop out back," he said, the words coming out before he could stop them. "He would lock the door."

Marc's coffee cup froze halfway to his mouth. Inside, silence stretched between them like glass about to shatter. Outside, traffic hummed, and a neighbor's radio drifted French pop music through the walls.

"I know," Marc said finally.

"What do you mean, you know?" Nick's voice came out sharp enough to make Marc flinch. "You *knew*?"

"*Mon dieu,*" Marc set his coffee down with shaking hands. "Everyone knew something was wrong. The way Gene would look at you boys, the way you both *changed*. You stopped talking, Jason started acting out. But your mother…" He trailed off.

Nick pushed himself to his feet, his coffee sloshing over the rim and scalding his hand. "My mother what?"

"She didn't want to see it. None of us did, really. It was easier to—"

"Easier?" Nick hurled the word like a weapon. "It was EASIER? I was twelve years old!"

Slumped back into the armchair, Marc was a far cry from the suave Parisian who had flirted with Nick only the night before. Now, he was an old man, living in a rundown apartment of hidden truths.

"And then," Nick's voice rose to fill the small space, "when Jason accused me—when he tried to tell someone in the only way he knew how—you all just… what? Shipped me off to Connecticut?"

"Nick, *s'il te plaît*. I had nothing to do with that."

"Did you know that's why he did it? Did you know that's why Jason hanged himself? Because the same man who hurt me, hurt him. Got away with ALL OF IT."

The neighbor's TV had gone silent. The whole building held its breath.

"Your mother," Marc started again, then stopped at the look on Nick's face.

"My mother is still in that hotel," Nick said, his voice deadly quiet now. "Planning to go to South Africa with her wife while her ex-husband's body gets cold and her dead son stays buried and her living son…" He laughed, the sound like something shattering. "Her living son fucks her friend to feel something."

Marc flinched as if he'd been slapped. "What do you mean, her friend?"

Nick met his eyes. "Don't pretend you don't know about Laslo."

"Laslo?" Marc's voice cracked. He stood up suddenly, moved to the barred window. "Last night, after dinner?"

"Does it matter when?"

"Of course it matters!" Marc spun around. "You were upset, you were vulnerable. I've never liked Laslo—he took advantage."

"Like you tried to?" Nick's voice was ice. "All those little touches last night? Those comments?"

Marc's face crumpled. "That was different. I was drunk. I was—"

Nick cut him off. "When I was a kid. You knew all of it was happening. And last night you still tried to—"

"Someone should have stopped it," Marc interrupted, his voice small. "Someone should have seen what was happening and stopped it."

"My mother, you mean?"

"The university," Marc said, still facing the window. "Lynne was respected. She was finally happy in her career. And then when she met Susan…"

"Everyone just looked away? Everyone just pretended not to notice while Gene destroyed two kids because what? It might have made things awkward at faculty parties?"

Marc's reflection in the window looked ancient, all his careful Parisian polish stripped away. "There were rumors," he said. "About students."

The room bucked beneath Nick's feet. "What?"

"Male students. Young ones. Nothing was ever proven, but some people said that Gene would sometimes sleep with his wife's—well, with your mother's students." Marc turned finally, his face grey. "Your mother protected him. She buried the complaints. She didn't want to believe—and they were university students, you know, over eighteen."

"Stop." Nick dragged his hands down his face. "Just... stop."

But Marc couldn't stop now. The words poured out like a confession. "When Jason made those accusations against you, Gene played it masterfully. He started dropping hints about how distance might help, how his colleague's son had benefited from a change of schools after 'similar troubles.' Your mother was already breaking under the pressure, and Gene knew exactly how to make her think that sending you away was her idea. 'For everyone's protection,' he'd said."

"It doesn't make sense," Nick said. "I mean, why would he want to protect *me*? Send me away, with what he was doing to me..."

"He'd had enough, *peut-être*?"

Nick flinched.

"I don't mean to hurt your feelings, *chéri*. But we can't try to make sense of people like him. And your mother? God, Lynne was so desperate for someone to tell her what to do—she latched onto it like a lifeline. Convinced herself she was being strong, making the hard choice to protect you. She never saw how Gene manipulated her, how he'd orchestrated the whole thing."

"And what about you?" Nick's voice was razor-sharp, quiet but cutting. "What was your role in all this? Standing on the sidelines? Taking notes for some future dinner party anecdote?"

Marc appeared to grow smaller as he spoke. "I attempted to have a conversation with your mother, back when everything happened with the suicide. She refused to listen. Claimed that I was being overdramatic and that Jason had always been difficult."

"Troubled," Nick repeated. The word hung in the stale air. "That's what they called me too, when they sent me to Aunt Julia's. Another troubled son. The difficult one."

"It didn't matter at that point, anyway."

"Didn't matter..."

"When Jason went off to that Bible college," Marc continued, his words coming faster now, "I knew. I knew the implications. I tried to tell Susan, but she was so focused on protecting your mother's happiness—"

"Susan knew?" The room contracted around Nick.

"She suspected. We all did. But your mother... she had finally found herself. Found love. Found a real life after Gene. We didn't want to..."

"To what?" Nick advanced on Marc. "To ruin her happiness with the small detail that her ex-husband was a predator? That he'd driven one son to suicide and the other to—" He stopped, choking on the words.

The neighbor's radio had resumed again, French pop floating through the walls like a mockery. Nick sat for another moment, then set his untouched coffee on the cluttered table and moved toward the door, his movements careful and deliberate, as if the slightest wrong step might shatter what little composure he had left.

3.

The key stuck in the lock. Nick forced the turn, metal biting into his palm. Inside, soft footsteps made him wonder if his own apartment meant to keep him out.

"Nick?" His mother's voice. Then Susan's murmur: "Let him come in first, Lynne."

He could turn around now, walk away, let them fly to Cape Town with their secrets. Instead, he pushed open the door.

They were sitting on his sofa—the same sofa where Laslo had… He stopped that thought. His mother looked small, her makeup perfect as always, but her hands gripping a glass of water. Susan stood by the window, her professor's posture rigid with tension.

"Marc called," Susan said. "The *gardienne* let us in. We said it was an emergency."

Nick let out a sarcastic laugh and let the door slam shut as he entered. The sound made his mother flinch.

"My boy," Lynne started, but Nick cut her off.

"Don't. Don't call me that. Not today." He remained standing at the door. Whatever charade he'd managed the night before—smiles, feints, calculated comments—had crumbled by morning. "Did you know what Gene was doing to Jason?"

The sudden question hit Lynne with the force of a punch. Her glass slipped from her hand, its contents spilling onto her pants. But she didn't register the cold seeping through the silk.

"Nick, please," Susan took a step forward. "Your mother's been through enough with Gene's death—"

"Enough?" Nick's laugh cut sharp enough to make both women wince. "What about what Jason went through? What about what *I* went through while everyone—" His voice cracked.

"While everyone just watched?"

"I didn't know." Lynne's eyes slid away. "I didn't want to know."

"Aunt Julia's," Nick said. "You let Gene isolate all of us from each other. You let him—"

"I was trying to protect you!" Lynne jolted upwards, water dripping from her pants. "Both of you! I thought if you were away from each other, away from him—"

"You weren't protecting us." Frost edged Nick's words. "You were protecting yourself."

"That's not fair," Susan said, but Nick rounded on her.

"Not fair? You suspected. Marc just told me. You all suspected. And you did nothing. You watched them send me away, watched Jason go off to that college, and you did nothing because what? Because you were in love with my mother? Because it was easier to pretend?"

"Stop," Lynne's voice cracked. "You don't understand what it was like. I was alone, I was scared."

"YOU were scared?" Nick's voice rose. "I was twelve years old! Jason was—" He stopped and wiped his hands across his face. When he spoke again, his voice was terrifyingly quiet. "Jason tried to tell someone. He tried to tell the church what Gene was doing, but he couldn't say it directly. So he accused me instead. And what did you do? You sent me away. You let Gene send me away."

"And now," Nick continued, dropping his hands, "now Gene gets to die without ever facing what he did. He gets an obituary calling him 'beloved.' While Jason is in the ground, and I'm—I'm still here, watching everyone pretend none of it ever happened."

"You don't understand," Lynne said again, but her voice had emptied of all defense. Only hollowness remained. "I did understand. I understood too well."

Susan's throat caught on a small, desperate noise, but Lynne pushed on: "I was nineteen when I met Gene. He was a friend of my older brother's, your uncle. Gene had been the family's auto mechanic." She sank back onto the couch. "He would drop by the house late in the evening. He'd asked to see my room. He would lock the door."

"Stop!" Nick cried out.

"I married him because I thought… I thought it would make it different. Make it real. Make it love instead of…" She held her hands to her mouth. "And then when I saw how he looked at you boys, I told myself I was imagining things. I told myself I was paranoid, that I was seeing things that weren't there because of my own history. I told myself—"

"But you knew. You knew exactly what was happening."

"I couldn't face it. I couldn't… If I admitted what he was doing to you, I'd have to admit what he'd done to me. What I'd let him do to Jason by staying silent. What I'd become by marrying him."

Susan stood still by the window, her face ash-white. Nick watched the shock ripple across her features and knew then that this truth—the extent of Gene's abuse, reaching back to Lynne's teenage years—had blindsided her just as much as him. All those years of half-told stories, of Lynne's careful editing of her past, suddenly made terrible sense. Susan had lived with shadows of this truth for years, glimpsing pieces but never seeing the full picture until now.

"So you sent me away," Nick said. The words echoed in the small apartment. "You sent me to Aunt Julia's when Jason tried to tell someone. You let him go off to that college. You just kept… moving us around like chess pieces to protect yourself."

"No," Lynne's hands were shaking violently now. "To protect you. Both of you. I thought… I thought if you were apart, if you were away from him…"

"But we weren't away from him, were we? We would never be *away* from him, not really, not in our minds—" He stopped, turned to Susan. "Did you know any of this?"

Susan looked like she might be sick. "Lynne never told me. Not everything, anyway. About Gene, about when she was young. But I knew something was wrong. The way she'd flinch sometimes when men got too close. The way she watched you boys like she was waiting for something terrible to happen."

"And you still let her send me away?" Nick asked.

"I didn't have the right." Shame tinged her words. "I wasn't your mother. I wasn't anyone's mother."

"No," Nick said. "You were just another adult who saw something wrong and did nothing."

Silence settled over the room, heavy as smoke in their throats. Lynne clamped her hands over her mouth as if forcibly holding back more terrible truths. Susan remained frozen by the window, her face pale and unreadable as she absorbed Lynne's revelation about Gene.

Lynne had told herself that sending Nick to Julia's was her decision, an act of maternal instinct. But now, decades later, her defense dissolved as easily as sugar in bitter coffee, leaving only the taste of doubt. Had she really chosen, or had she simply followed Gene's carefully laid breadcrumbs? "Some distance might be good for everyone," she'd said, unwittingly echoing Gene's words. She'd been so proud of her strength in making that choice, never seeing how Gene had shaped her thoughts, suggested solutions that served his own ends. Protection, she'd told herself. But protection for whom?

"I need air." Nick's words came out strangled. All the lies caught like soot in his lungs.

"Jason wrote to you," Lynne said, the words falling out like she couldn't hold them anymore.

Nick's mouth turned dry, and his throat grew more and more constricted. "What?"

"He wrote a letter. To you. When he was fifteen or sixteen. He didn't have your address, so he gave it to me to send to you." Lynne, avoiding Nick's eye, spoke to her own hands instead.

The floor seemed to tilt under Nick's feet. "I never got any letter."

"I kept it." The words came small and broken. "I told myself I was protecting you. That you were finally settling in, finally starting to smile again. I told myself reading his letter would only… upset you."

Nick stood rooted in place, unable to move. Each breath scraped against the walls of his throat.

"You kept his letter." His voice came rough, each word cutting like glass in his mouth. "For all those years, while I thought he hated me, while I thought he'd accused me because he was cruel, because he wanted to hurt me… you had his letter."

"Nick," Susan started, but he cut her off.

"Where is it now?"

Lynne's eyes swiveled toward him with unsettling precision, her face tear-streaked but her makeup still perfect. Always perfect. "In my purse. In the blue wallet. I've carried it with me every time I've traveled. Every new city, every new life. Like some kind of…" She laughed, a horrible sound. "Some kind of penance, I suppose."

"I want to read it," Nick said. "Now."

Lynne balanced on the sofa's edge, eyes fixed on him, while Susan claimed the doorway as her post. Finally, Lynne knelt, unzipped her handbag, and pulled out her wallet. From it, she withdrew a thin, folded sheet of paper, yellowed and frayed at the edges. Taking the letter, Nick sank into the oversized armchair, crushing the paper's edges as he read.

4.

Hey Nick,

I hope Aunt Julia is treating you alright. Mom says you're doing better there, that you're getting good grades and making friends. I don't know if that's true or if she's just trying to make herself feel better. She talks about you a lot but in this weird way, like she's describing someone else's kid. Like you're this character in a story she's telling.

I keep trying to write this letter. I've started it like five times now. There's stuff I need to tell you but I don't know how. Every time I try the words come out wrong. My hands shake and I feel sick to my stomach and I end up throwing the paper away and starting over. This is attempt number 6. Maybe this time I'll actually mail it.

Dad bought me a car. Can you believe that? A piece of crap Hyundai but still. He says it's because, when I get my license, I need to be able to drive myself to youth group and basketball practice, but really I think it's because he wants me to stop asking to visit you. Each time I ask, he keeps saying how expensive plane tickets are or how complicated it would be to arrange everything. But he can buy a car no problem. That's Dad though, right? I think maybe the car was a way to show mom that he's doing fine without her.

Remember that time we were playing that old Sega Genesis in the basement and Dad came down and said he needed to show you something outside in his workshop? And how after you came back you wouldn't play Aladdin anymore? You just sat there staring at the screen while I kept playing? I didn't understand then because Aladdin was your favorite game. You liked how Aladdin would run with that monkey around the screen and collect apples. But I think maybe I do get it now. There were a lot of times like that. Times that I didn't understand and now I can't stop thinking about. It's like someone turned on a light and now I can see everything that was happening in the dark and I wish I could turn it off again.

The youth pastor keeps asking me to give my testimony at church. About how God helped me overcome my "false witness" against you. That's what they're calling it. False witness. Like I'm just some kid who made up lies about his brother. Dad encouraged it, of course. Told everyone how concerned he was about my spiritual state, about my "tendency toward deception." He's got everyone at church thinking he's this amazing Christian father, dealing with his troubled sons and his wife, who turned into a lesbian. Makes me want to scream sometimes.

I started going to this new fast food joint after school. They opened it where the McDonald's used to be. It's kind of a dump but they don't care if you sit there for hours just drinking one Coke. There's a guy that works there named Mike who's probably your age. Sometimes he sits with me when it's slow and we talk about music and books and stuff. He can tell something's wrong, I think. Keeps telling me I can talk to him if I need to. But how do you even start that conversation? How do you tell someone that your whole life is built on secrets and you don't know how to keep carrying the lies?

I'm sorry I was such a dick to you when we were little. And I'm sorry I said those things about you at church. I'm sorry they sent you away. I didn't know what else to do. I thought if I told them about you maybe they'd figure out about everything else. About him. But they didn't understand what I was trying to say and now you're gone and it's all messed up and I don't know how to fix it. Sometimes I dream about just getting in that stupid car and driving to Connecticut. Just showing up at Aunt Julia's door. But then what would I say? Would you even want to see me?

Dad says you don't want to hear from me. Maybe that's true. Maybe you hate me now and maybe you should.

Jason

P.S. I found the Sega Genesis in a box in the basement last week. Still had Aladdin inside. I've been playing at night when I can't sleep. It's stupid but it makes me feel less lonely.

5.

"Did you read this?" Nick asked without looking up. "All these years, have you read it?"

"Over and over," Lynne said. "Until I had it memorized."

Nick ran his fingers over the soft and worn paper, feeling the creases and edges that held his brother's story. He could almost imagine the imprints left by his mother's fingers, proof of the countless times she had read and reread the letter. His brother's messy teenage handwriting swam before his eyes: "Remember that time we were playing that old Sega Genesis in the basement…"

Twice, Nick had paused reading, overwhelmed by the specific details from Jason's letter. The workshop reference hit first, flooding back the sharp tang of motor oil and tools and the gritty air. Then came Aladdin, his favorite game, and the memories fully broke through: His fingers held the memory of the smooth plastic controller, his eyes the bright sweep of that monkey snatching apples across the screen.

When he reached the part about the youth pastor, about "false witness," his mother made a sound like something breaking in her throat—and in that break, Nick heard twenty years of guilt pouring out. He looked at the P.S. again, about the Sega Genesis. Jason playing Aladdin alone at night. "And you never thought… You never thought I should see this?"

"I convinced myself the letter would only hurt you more," Lynne said. Her voice sounded far away. "That you were finally doing better at Julia's, that dragging it all up again would only…"

"Doing better?" Nick barked out a sound that barely passed for laughter. "Is that what you told yourself? That I was doing better?"

"It had been so many years..."

Susan moved from her post by the door, took a step toward him, but Nick held up his hand to stop her.

He had to give his mother some credit: Aunt Julia's house had been a refuge. Julia, with her quiet ways and steady love. Julia, whose home had never known Gene's footsteps.

"The workshop," he said, the words hollow as old bones. "He mentions the workshop. Did you ever wonder why? Did you ever think about what happened out there?"

"Nick—" Lynne started.

"He knew," Nick said. "All that time, Jason knew. He was trying to tell someone, trying to tell everyone, but none of you would listen. And now he's dead, and this..." he held up the letter, "this is all that's left."

6.

Nick climbed the narrow stairs to Laslo's studio, each step echoing in the stairwell. His shirt clung to his back from sweat, and Jason's letter burned in his pocket. With each step, Nick rehearsed what he would say to Laslo. About taking advantage. About betrayal. About how everyone in his life gave the impression of watching and doing nothing.

The building crouched near the Bastille, an old artist's residence with floors that slanted and walls that met at impossible angles. Paint peeled from the walls in brittle strips, exposing decades of color choices like rings in a tree. Nick squeezed past a bike chained to the banister, its rusted frame leaving an orange streak across his shirt.

He could hear classical music as he reached the top floor. Something baroque, precise, filtering through the gap beneath Laslo's door. Light spilled onto the landing, painting a golden rectangle on the scarred floorboards.

The letter had hollowed him out. He'd read it once, twice—then again without really seeing the words. What it meant unraveled inside him too quickly to name. By the time he had left his mother and Susan, Lynne had gone silent, and Susan had said his name like a question.

But Nick hadn't answered. He needed something real. Something now.

Now he stood at Laslo's door, hand raised to knock, suddenly unsure. Then, through the door's frosted glass panel, Nick saw movement: Laslo's silhouette passing back and forth, pausing, moving again. The same way he'd moved last night, in Nick's apartment, deliberate and graceful even in that moment of desperate connection.

Nick's hand clenched around Jason's letter. He had come for answers, for confrontation, for some kind of closure. But as he stood there, watching Laslo's silhouette shift behind the frosted glass, another truth settled over him—he had come hoping Laslo would convince him it wasn't true. That there was some explanation, some way to make everything right again. The realization turned his stomach sour.

Before he could talk himself out of it, Nick pushed the door open.

The studio hit him at the threshold—just a converted attic, smaller than his mind had built it, where late afternoon light spilled through angled windows. Between the forest of easel legs, canvases lined the walls like undivulged secrets. The air carried its own history: sharp linseed oil, biting turpentine, and beneath those, the deeper notes of tobacco, wine, and long hours spent alone.

Laslo stood at an easel near the furthest window, his brush frozen mid-stroke. He wore a paint-stained shirt, rolled to the elbows…

Nick forced any thoughts of the previous night away. "Nice music," he said, swallowing the arguments he'd rehearsed. "Bach?"

"Handel, actually." Laslo set the brush down with exaggerated care, as if handling something that might explode. "The Messiah. Part III. The less famous bits." Unmoving, he let the precise baroque phrases fill the awkward space between them.

The studio's tall windows caught the afternoon sun, and long fingers stretched across the paint-splattered floor. Empty wine bottles lined one windowsill, their green glass turning emerald where the light passed through. A half glass of red sat beside Laslo's current canvas.

"I need to talk to you about last night," Nick began, but his voice caught as his eyes adjusted to the room. The paintings. They were everywhere, dozens of them, maybe hundreds, stacked against walls, arranged on easels, some just propped against each other on the floor. And they were all…

"That looks like a basement," he said, stepping toward the nearest canvas. The scene emerged from layers of dark oil: Two boys, bathed in the television's blue light, shared a sagging couch. Behind them stretched a doorway, black as a throat. The smaller boy hunched forward, captivated by his game, while the older one… Nick's stomach knotted. He knew that rigid posture, those watching eyes fixed on the darkness behind them.

"You and Jason," Laslo said quietly. "Playing that game you loved. The Genie, wasn't it?"

Nick felt Jason's letter crinkle in his pocket. "Aladdin. How did you…"

"I've been painting these scenes for years," Laslo continued. "Sometimes from memories. Sometimes from things Susan let slip. Sometimes from just… watching." He motioned to another canvas. The scene showed the Seine at night, a lone figure standing by the rail. "I saw you there sometimes, just staring at the water. You looked so much like Jason used to look." His fingers skimmed the edge of one canvas, almost a caress. "I kept my distance—knew you wouldn't want to see me—but I couldn't stop watching. Couldn't stop painting. You never noticed me, but I was there. Always there."

Nick stared at the painting until Laslo's meaning emerged. There Nick stood on the riverbank, his form barely contained by blues and blacks, bleeding into the darkness of the water below. Then he saw it—the other presence, the watcher in the background. Gene. Of course Gene would be in Nick's painting. He'd infected every scene, every moment, reaching across an ocean to haunt even this Paris night.

"The darkness here," Laslo said, gesturing at the Seine, "it has its own rules. The way it catches the light, how it can make people disappear. I can never quite paint it right. But that night, the way you stood there…" His voice faded as he moved to the next canvas.

Nick's skin grew cold as he understood. His darkest moments by the Seine—moments he'd thought were his alone—Laslo had been there, watching, collecting. Each painting peeled back another layer of privacy. How many other nights had those artist's eyes followed him, transforming his private grief into public display?

The paintings trapped him, one after another. A workshop at twilight, tools lined up on the bench with terrible precision, a small baseball cap dropped on the floor. A closed door leaking light beneath. Two bikes abandoned in tall grass, rust climbing their chains. An old Ford truck rotting in a driveway, weeds threading through its wheels.

Nick moved deeper into the studio. The space organized itself in concentric circles, like Dante's rings of hell, each area darker and more revealing than the last. The classical music followed him, Handel's precise harmonies a jarring counterpoint to the visual chaos. Through the open windows, the scent of someone's supper drifted up from the café below—garlic and herbs suffocated this private gallery of nightmares with the smell of memory turned sour.

Near the edges of the room, propped against the floorboards and ceramic heaters, Laslo's paintings were smaller, more tentative. Some were painted in cheap acrylics on what appeared to be cardboard boxes, Laslo's impatience too urgent to wait for proper canvases. A Fourth of July barbecue in an ordinary backyard—everyone gathered around a grill, nameless faces rendered in paint. The composition caught Nick's eye: There stood Gene, set apart from the group and turned toward the playground where two boys pushed each other on the swings. His pose looked casual enough, one hand tucked in his pocket, but his shadow—reaching, hungry, clawing its way across the grass toward the boys—betrayed him.

Another canvas showed their Missouri kitchen at Christmas. Wrapping paper scattered across the floor, new toys lay half-unpacked in their boxes. But Laslo had painted the window light wrong, too sharp, throwing stark blades across everything. Looming in the foreground, Gene was pictured darker than everything else, as if Laslo had mixed different paint for him, something denser, something that absorbed all the light in the room.

Even smaller canvases lined the wall, each showing ordinary moments that Laslo's brush twisted into something ominous: Nick and Jason bent over homework at the kitchen table while Gene's reflection lurked in the darkened window. The boys playing in the garden, but seen from the viewer's position inside the workshop, a perspective that turned their familiar sibling ritual into something furtive and watched. A church picnic spread out in summer colors—checkered tablecloths, bowls of potato salad—but Gene's hand gripped Nick's shoulder while Jason turned away, his face a mask of studied ignorance.

"These are from photographs," Laslo said, following Nick's gaze. "Your mother used to show them at faculty parties. Such a perfect family, everyone said. But look—" He moved closer to one of the church picnic paintings. "Look at how the light falls. How the shadows never quite match the sun's position. I was trying to show how nothing was quite how it appeared."

Nick stepped closer to a larger canvas. Their house at twilight, every window lit from within like a dollhouse. The lights in the upstairs windows had been painted in sickly yellow, but the workshop's single bulb glowed an unnatural red, a red that made Nick's stomach clench with remembering.

"I didn't understand at first," Laslo continued. "I just knew something was wrong with the light. Something was wrong with everything."

Nick drifted forward, drawn against his will to a wall of almost minuscule paintings, some no bigger than an index card, each one a window into a moment he'd tried to forget. The canvases were arranged chronologically, he realized—he could track his own growth from picture to picture, watch himself shrink into himself year by year while Jason's figure grew sharper, angrier, more defined. Laslo's technique evolved too, becoming more precise as his understanding deepened, as if the truth bled through canvas after canvas, demanding to be seen.

"I started painting these when I first moved to Paris," Laslo said, following behind Nick. "After that year in Missouri, after everything I'd witnessed but hadn't fully understood. At first, they were just scenes, moments I'd observed during faculty gatherings, dinners, department meetings. But the more I painted, the more I began to see what I'd been blind to while I was there."

"When was this?" Nick stopped in front of a canvas showing their old kitchen in Missouri. Through the window, you could see him and Jason playing in the yard, while Gene watched from the back door. Nick recognized the angle at once—this was painted by someone sitting at their own kitchen table, watching.

"Spring of ninety-nine. That particular dinner was during a heat wave, I think. By then, I'd been a regular fixture at the house for months. Susan was there too, as she increasingly was.

Everyone still called her your mother's 'friend,' but by then, the act was getting harder to keep up." Laslo released an empty laugh. "I spent that whole evening watching Gene watch you boys. The way his eyes followed you. I told myself I was imagining things, but it made for a good point of reference. Artists—we are always looking for material, for inspiration."

Now Nick ventured a little further into the studio's space. Next to the toilet, Laslo had stacks of canvases piled on one another. Nick flicked through them, each sinister, more explicit in its implications than the previous works. Here were the basement scenes: Nick and Jason on the couch, their faces drowned in the blue TV glow. And then some more scenes in a workshop: household tools scattered all across the surfaces, a small T-shirt discarded by the door. Moments Nick recognized with visceral clarity. And in these, Laslo had begun to paint himself into the backgrounds—a figure at a window, a shadow in a doorway, always watching, never intervening.

"You were there," Nick said, stopping in front of a painting of a church picnic. In it, he could see himself, around thirteen, sitting alone at a table. His younger self picked at a paper plate of macaroni and cheese, while in the background Laslo stood with a drink in his hand, his face a mask of helpless knowledge. "All those years, you were there."

"I was always there," Laslo said, the words catching in his throat. "Not… physically. Missouri only gave me half a year. But I never stopped watching, in my own way. Always trying to glean from Susan whatever I could, bits and pieces of the stories from her past that Lynne would tell her. Always telling myself someone else would stop it, someone else would speak up. Always finding reasons not to be the one who…" He trailed off, moving to the window where the wine bottles stood like green watchmen. "Would you like a drink?"

"No," Nick said, remembering last night. The wine, the touches, the desperate attempt to feel something other than numbness. "I want to see the rest."

Nick's breath caught at the next stack of paintings. Laslo's style had turned surgical in its detail, each canvas rendered with photographic clarity. There Gene dangled the truck keys from one finger. There Jason froze at the bus station, his backpack slipping off his shoulder as Gene filled the entrance.

And in each painting, Laslo's self-portrait became more prominent, more tortured. In one scene, he stood in their driveway, watching Gene lead Nick to the workshop, his hands clenched into fists at his sides. In another, he sat in a pew at church, head bowed not in prayer but in shame as Jason spoke to the youth pastor.

"When did you paint these?" Nick asked, his voice strange in the shadowy studio. The setting sun streamed through the tall windows, stretching dark patterns across the floor and sparking new, ghoulish life into the paintings.

"After Jason died," Laslo said. He had already downed his entire glass of wine. "I couldn't stop. It was like… like I had to document everything I'd failed to prevent. Every moment I'd witnessed and done nothing about."

They edged further along. Here, the paintings became almost unbearable. Jason at the Bible college, standing alone in a dormitory hallway, his face a mask of despair. The phone calls Nick never knew about—Jason in a phone booth, receiver clutched to his ear, while in the background Gene's car idled in the parking lot.

"Artists," Laslo said softly, "we tell ourselves we're just observing, just collecting material. But we're really just professional cowards, aren't we? Turning other people's pain into pictures."

Nick could taste acid at the back of his throat. A whole year of his and Jason's lives, documented, archived, and turned into art, while no one had done anything to help. But no, some of these paintings were newer, more intimate, more unguarded.

"But some of these are later, when you left. How could you possibly—?"

Laslo's voice dropped low as he moved toward a stack of canvases propped against the wall. "Jason talked to me. It was the summer after his high school graduation. He showed up at my door with a backpack and those eyes that wouldn't settle. The summer before he went off to Bible college. He'd sit right where you're standing now, sometimes for hours. At first, he just watched me paint. Then he started talking."

Laslo lifted a canvas: Jason bent over his notebook in a Saint-Germain café, the perspective so close Nick could almost read the words.

"He wrote all the time. Pages and pages. Sometimes he'd share fragments—always about childhood. The workshop. You."

Nick's head jerked up. "What?! Jason was never in Paris." The words left his mouth sharp with certainty. But even as he spoke, his mind wavered. The years gaped with holes: his time at Aunt Julia's, then university, and his early days in Paris when news of home came only through Lynne's scattered updates.

"Six days," Laslo said, pulling out another canvas. This one showed the Pont Neuf at twilight, Jason leaning over the bridge.

Nick took a step back, his pulse hammering. "No. No, that's not possible. I—I would have known." But would he? How many times had he ignored his brother's calls? Left messages unanswered? He had been too busy—moving money around, building a future as far away from his past as possible.

"He kept saying he had to find you, had to tell you something. But you were moving, busy becoming somebody." Laslo's fingers, a gentle whisper, skimmed the edge of one canvas. "He was different in Paris," Laslo said, moving to another canvas. "Different from how I remembered him as a child in Missouri. And he kept saying he had to find you, had to tell you something," Laslo continued. "He used to watch the bank where you worked from across the street. Just... waiting... hoping you'd come out, I suppose."

Nick gripped the edge of a nearby worktable, knuckles whitening. Jason had been in Paris. Not just passing through—but searching for him. Watching. Waiting. And Nick had never known.

The paintings from this period were different—more immediate, raw. Jason smoking on a balcony, his face half-turned away. Jason asleep on what looked like Laslo's couch, a journal fallen open beside him. Jason in the Luxembourg Gardens, surrounded by children playing while he sat alone, still and watchful.

"He was lost," Laslo continued. "Desperate for someone to understand. To see him." His fingers skimmed the edge of one canvas, almost a caress. "We spent a lot of time together that week. Perhaps too much time." He motioned to another canvas. Here, Jason was in a nightclub, the strobe lights catching his face in a moment of wild abandon. "He'd dance for hours, then crash on my couch, talking until dawn."

Nick swallowed hard against the nausea. His brother—fractured, clever, and impossible to reach—had been here, in this very space, confiding in Laslo while he, Nick, had remained oblivious.

"Your couch?" he echoed.

"He needed a safe place." Laslo's voice turned defensive.

"Lynne believed he was at a hostel, but he couldn't face being alone in a place like that."

Laslo pulled out the next painting, and Nick's breath left him in a ragged exhale. Jason, curled on the sofa, his bare back a canvas of its own. Every bruise stood out with sickening distinctness.

Nick's stomach lurched, the threat of vomit imminent. "Did you...?" He couldn't finish the question.

Laslo grimaced. "No," he bit out. "Never. But he wanted... he needed..." He stopped, ran a hand through his hair, then started again. "He kept trying to make connections. With strangers in bars. With boys his age at cafés. With anyone who might understand without him having to explain."

Nick swallowed hard, his vision blurring at the edges. He had spent years believing he had been the one abandoned. Now, faced with the evidence of Jason's silent search, he felt the weight of something far worse.

He had been the one who hadn't seen.

Laslo turned a larger canvas facing the wall. Nick glimpsed Jason at the kitchen table, morning light making a child of him again, Laslo's oversized shirt hanging from his shoulders—and had to turn away.

"I don't even think Jason was *homosexual*," Laslo said, frowning. "He just desired—desired... to be desired."

Nick tensed; he had often wondered the same about himself—whether his feelings for other men were truly love or longing, or simply a search for comfort.

"The last night," Laslo said, his voice thin, "Jason tried to kiss me. Said he needed to know if touch could ever mean something different. Something not violent." He looked at Nick. "I stopped him. Sent him back to Missouri the next day. Two months later..."

"Two months later he died," Nick said. The words fell like stones into the murky studio.

"He left his journal here," Laslo said. "I found it under the couch after. I tried to get it to you, but your mother..." He moved toward his desk, started opening drawers.

"Don't," Nick said. "I don't want to see it."

Laslo reached for a spiral notebook, warped from use. "Your name ran through every page. His guilt about what he did to you. How he fed that lie to the church because he saw no other way to make you both safe."

The paintings around them pulsed in the fading light—Jason at the Louvre, staring up at dark religious scenes. Jason in the Tuileries, watching children play. Jason at Laslo's window, the Seine reflecting in the glass, doubling his haunted expression.

"The night he tried to... the night I sent him away," Laslo's voice caught. "He said something I've never forgotten. He said, 'Nick got away. He got to Aunt Julia's, got free. But I'm still in that workshop every night in my dreams.'"

Nick felt his legs start to give out. He grabbed the edge of a table, sending paint tubes rolling to the floor.

"I should have helped him," Laslo continued. "Should have done something more than just... document everything. But I thought if I could just show what was happening, someone would finally see. Someone would finally understand."

"You saw him," Nick said. "You saw him here, alive, trying to tell someone what happened. While I was... While I was pretending to be someone else entirely. You should have tried to get in touch, or *he* should have tried. I—I don't know."

The studio had grown darker, but Nick could still make out the progression of paintings. Jason getting thinner with each portrayal, more desperate, more haunted. His face taking on the same wasted look Nick saw in his own mirror that morning.

"Maybe you blame Lynne, but I believe the Bible college was Gene's idea," Laslo said, his voice thick with loathing. "When Gene found out about Paris," Laslo said, his voice tightening, "I got a call from your mother. She was hysterical. Gene had tracked Jason's credit card charges, found the flights, all the receipts. He'd told Gene that he was going to a summer camp. And Gene seized on the betrayal as final proof that Jason needed 'guidance.' That's when he insisted on him going to that school." Laslo moved to another canvas, this one showing Jason bent over college application forms, Gene's shadow looming in the doorway. "No discussion, no gap year, no other options. By September, Jason was enrolled. Two months later..." He stopped, his hand frozen over the painting's surface. "Two months was all it took."

Nick remembered the letter in his pocket, Jason's words about Gene's "concern" for his spiritual state. The pieces were assembling themselves into an unbearable picture. Nick understood now: desperation, not just depression, had taken Jason's life. His last escape from a trap that had been closing since that Paris summer, since Gene had stripped away every other option, every other path to freedom. The official story had been neat, clean: troubled boy, spiritual crisis, tragic end. But the truth had more edges—a summer of freedom in Paris, perhaps a desperate attempt to warn his brother, then the suffocating walls of Bible college closing in until only one door remained unopened.

"I painted him one last time," Laslo said. "From memory. Just after I found out that he'd died." He moved to a small canvas tucked behind others. "I've never shown this to anyone."

A simple scene: Jason's empty dorm room bathed in morning light, dust dancing in the air. Only the shadow gave the painting meaning—a boy's silhouette stretched across the floor toward the door, reaching, always reaching, for what remained forever beyond his grasp.

"Stop," Nick shouted, but Laslo couldn't halt the flow of canvases now, each one a fresh wound.

"After that, I started seeing him everywhere. In your face whenever I caught a glimpse of you in the city. Paris is small, after all. And it's in the way you move, the way you hold yourself apart from everyone." Laslo's hands were shaking as he turned the canvases around. "I kept painting you both. Together, separate. The same pain wearing different faces."

The innermost ring of paintings tracked Nick through Paris—real moments tangled with Laslo's fevered visions. Nick on midnight bridges, staring into the Seine's black waters. Nick jerking away from passing servers at café tables. But Gene haunted every canvas: an apparition in glass, a reflection in water, a specter that followed even here, an ocean away.

"Your faces blur together sometimes," Laslo said, moving closer. "When I paint. When I drink. When I…" He gestured to the wet canvas on the easel. "Last night, in your apartment, I kept seeing him. The same desperation. The same need to prove something about touch, about connection."

"Last night," Nick said, before his voice died. The final painting waited on the easel, oils still wet. In it, Nick's apartment, the sofa where he and Laslo had… His eyes caught on Gene looming in the doorway, watching. And Laslo had sketched in his own face too—caught in a look of guilt that answered Gene's dark pleasure.

"Jason would sit where you are now," Laslo said. "Talking about you. About how you were the strong one, the one who got away. He didn't understand that you'd just found a different kind of prison."

The studio contracted around Nick, its scent thick with turpentine and revelation. His heart hammered in the silence—the music had stopped, abandoning him to the city sounds below. Traffic hummed, plates clinked in the café, life went on while his world collapsed canvas by canvas.

"Jason was here," Nick said, still staring at the wet painting. "In Paris. And none of you told me. And him. He's to blame too. He could have called. Could have..."

"Could he? Would you have answered?"

The walls of paintings closed further in. Nick could feel them all around him—every scene, every moment, every violation witnessed and documented.

"Do you know what he said that last night?" Laslo moved closer still. "After I stopped him from... after I sent him away? He said, 'Nick was right to leave. To forget all of us. Some things you can't paint over.'"

"And this?" Nick gestured to the wet painting, unable to face it now. "What is this supposed to be?"

"What I saw," Laslo said, his voice raw. "What I always see. Him. Always him. In every room, every moment. Even last night..."

"Stop." Nick hit a wall of canvases. He could no longer breathe, boxed in by painted horrors. Gene stared back from every angle, the workshop's red light pulsing through frame after frame. "You had no right. Any of it. Taking in Jason, feeding him hope night after night. Making him think you could save him. Making me—"

Someone in the building slammed a door, making them both jump. Laslo reached for a lamp, but Nick stopped him.

"Don't. I don't want to see anymore. I don't want to see how you've been... collecting us. Collecting our pain like it's some kind of… of art project. You let him sit here night after night, telling you everything, and all you did was paint. Paint him. Like Gene watching through that workshop window."

"You don't understand," Laslo said, his voice tight. "I tried to help him. To understand what he was telling me. But he was like you—always dancing around the truth, always speaking in code."

"Why did you really come to my apartment last night?"

The night had become absolute now, the paintings just shapes around them. Nick could sense Laslo moving closer, could smell wine and paint and something else—the same cologne he'd worn all those years ago, when Nick had just been a boy hiding under tables at faculty parties.

"I needed to see."

"See what?"

"How it would end."

Nick took a step backward, bumped into a canvas. It clattered to the floor. "What would end?"

"The story. Your story. Jason's story." Laslo's voice came from somewhere closer now. "I've painted everything else. Every moment. Every attempt at escape. But I needed the ending."

"I'm not a story." Nick's back hit the wall. "We weren't your subjects. We weren't Gene's subjects. We were just kids."

"Aren't you?" Closer still. Nick could smell the wine on Laslo's breath, could almost feel the heat of his body in the darkness. "Isn't that what we all were to Gene? Just pictures he could arrange? Just scenes he could compose? Even Jason understood that, in the end. Why do you think he chose that particular way to die? Creating his final tableau?"

"Stay back."

"That's what you said last night. Right before you didn't."

Somewhere a siren wailed, its light flashing through the windows, illuminating Laslo's face inches from Nick's. In that strobing moment, Nick saw the same expression Laslo had painted on Gene in a dozen canvases—that mixture of desire and dominance that made Nick's stomach turn.

"You're just like him," Nick said.

"No." Laslo's hand found Nick's cheek in the dark, the same way he'd touched Jason on that morning—after painting. "He at least believed his own lies. I knew exactly what I was doing. With Jason. With you. Creating my own perfect scenes."

Nick knocked Laslo's hand away. "Don't touch me."

"But you let me last night." Laslo's voice, thick with something between desire and disgust, broke through the blackness. "Let me make you into art. Just like Jason wanted to, that last night here. Both of you, seeking validation in all the wrong places."

"Shut up!" Nick could feel the wet canvas behind him, Gene's painted eyes watching. Desperate to escape this confession, he grasped in the shadows for a light switch.

"Such a perfect scene," Laslo mused, his voice turning cold with artistic detachment. "The broken son, reaching for comfort in the wrong embrace. Just as Jason did, when he—"

The crack of knuckles against jaw came before thought. Laslo crashed into an easel, and the paintings followed—Jason writing at the café, Jason staring from the bridge, Jason wrapped in Laslo's clothes. Each captured moment of false sanctuary slamming to the paint-flecked floor.

"Don't say his name." Nick's voice was loose gravel. "You don't get to say his name. Not after you let him pour out his soul here night after night while you just… watched. Another pair of eyes seeing everything, doing nothing."

Laslo laughed, a horrible sound in the darkness. "Hit me again. It'll make such a beautiful painting. 'Son Confronts Witness.' Or should I call it 'Like Father, Like—'"

This time Nick grabbed him by the shirt collar, slammed him against the wall. Paint tubes crunched under their feet. The smell of turpentine rose sharp and toxic, mixing with Laslo's cologne, with the lingering scent of wine.

"Is that what you want?" Nick's breath hit Laslo's face. "More material for your sick collection? Another betrayal to paint?"

"At least I made something beautiful," Laslo's voice floated, almost dreamy. "At least I showed the truth, even if I couldn't stop it. Even if I couldn't save Jason. Save you."

Nick had Laslo pinned against the wall now, one arm tight against his throat. The position struck him with sickening familiarity—Gene's preferred method of persuasion. Through the windows, the city lights caught the fallen paintings, all those captured moments of pain and observation mixing together on the floor.

And then, a memory took form—a memory he had tried to bury. He had been eleven, just before everything truly began. Gene's temper was as sharp as ever, a storm summoned by the slightest provocation. That day, Nick hadn't thought he was the intended target of his father's fury. Yet somehow, he had ended up at its very center.

The scene unfolded in his bedroom, once a sanctuary. Lying on his bed, he had been staring up at the ceiling as he had countless times before. In another room, screams and shouts flew back and forth between Lynne and Gene, not unlike what happened most weekends. But then, from nowhere, the door was framed by the looming figure of his father. The hands that Nick had watched so many times—hands that could coax engines back to life, that could strip and rebuild carburetors with surgical precision, that could find the source of any whine or whisper—became something else. Those mechanic fingers, still dark with motor oil under the nails, wrapped around his throat with the same methodical certainty they applied to broken machines. In that moment, the world contracted to a singular point of tension, and Nick understood with terrible clarity that his father saw no difference between hands that fixed engines and hands that exacted anger. Here was a man who was supposed to be his protector, his guide—now transformed into a source of inexplicable terror.

No matter how he tried to bury the memory, it left indelible marks on the landscape of Nick's life. That moment of violation—of violence—shaped his relationships, his perception of trust, and his understanding of love. Like a chapter in his story he wished had never been written, its narrative intertwined with his own, molding the person he had become.

The memory gained its sharpest contours when he recalled his mother, standing in the bedroom doorway. Tears streaked her face as she pleaded with his father, her voice filling the space between them. But Nick couldn't remember her stepping forward, couldn't recall her hands prying his father's away.

Amid the chaos of Laslo's studio, a chilling clarity settled over Nick. From that moment in the bedroom, he'd stopped struggling, ceased his attempts to free himself. Maybe that act of surrender had reached his father—perhaps the sight of his own child motionless beneath him, the absence of resistance where there had once been a desperate fight. In any case, Gene finally let go. The hands that had been instruments of harm just seconds ago withdrew, leaving behind their lingering sensation on Nick's throat.

Panting for breath, Nick had coursed with a surge of emotions: relief intertwined with confusion, anger tangled with despair. No victory—just an escape from an unthinkable moment.

Nick could finally see that day as a turning point, the moment Gene started testing boundaries, seeing what he could get away with. Within months, the workshop became his favorite place to assert control, and Nick's twelfth year became the dividing line between before and after.

Now, with his own arm against Laslo's throat, Nick felt the cycle completing itself. He could feel Laslo's pulse against his forearm, rabbit-fast. Could smell the wine and dusted canvases and fear. His free hand already curled into a fist. It would be so easy. So tragic. Just the kind of scene Laslo lived to paint.

Then he saw their reflection in the window: two dark figures, one pinning the other. Just like in Laslo's paintings. Just like in his memories of Gene. Just like in that last painting of Jason in the dorm room, reaching forever toward an escape he never found.

Nick let go with such intensity that Laslo slid down the wall, gasping. "You can't paint what happens next," Nick said, his voice steady despite the growing pain in his forehead. "You don't get to document this part."

He stepped back, careful not to touch any of the canvases. The room had grown smaller, sadder. Just an old artist's studio full of stolen moments and secondhand pain.

"Nick," Laslo started, still on his knees.

"No." Nick found the door in the dark. "You've had enough of me."

He let the stairwell, nearly obscured by the night, swallow him. From behind, Laslo tended to his fallen art—frames scraping floor, canvases shuffling into order. Nick's steps quickened at the sound: Gene's workshop ritual of straightening tools, making order of chaos.

The street hit him with its ordinary cacophony: traffic noise, tourists' laughter, the smell of fresh bread from the boulangerie on the corner. Too much. Too real. His mind lurched sideways, seeking escape, and he then was elsewhere: standing on a granite cliff face, grey rock stretching endlessly in both directions. Before him, an ocean vast and colorless as blank paper. No boats disturbed its surface. No birds wheeled overhead. Just the sea breathing in and out like something alive and waiting. The air tasted of salt and absence—clean, untouched by memory or pain. Here, he could disappear into the silence between waves. Here, where even the wind held its breath, he could imagine stepping off the edge and finding not death but transformation. The possibility hung before him like an open door.

A car horn shattered the vision. Nick found himself still in Paris, his hand pressed against rough stone, steadying himself outside Laslo's building. The sea lingered in his mind, that grey infinity with its promise of erasure. But his feet remained planted on the sidewalk, his body anchored by the weight of Jason's letter in his pocket. Some escapes were only temporary. Some doors, once opened, couldn't be closed again.

7.

Life spilled onto the sidewalks, the humid air filled with the smells of garlic and wine and the sounds of common, everyday joy. A couple brushed past, the woman's laughter mixing with her clicking heels, the man's hand resting easily on her back. Their easy intimacy scraped Nick raw after Laslo's gallery of stolen moments.

Jason's letter crumpled under his fingers in his pocket. Those paintings upstairs, they'd missed the truth. Not one had captured what these worn pages held: what Jason had tried to say.

His phone buzzed with Susan's texts:

"Your mother's asking for you."

"Are you okay?"

"Nick?"

"I didn't know about the paintings."

The last message hit hardest. Laslo had gotten to her first.

Place de la Bastille opened before him; the July Column rose like a silent rebuke. Tourists posed for photos, their faces lit by the column's golden glow. A group of English-speaking students sat on the steps and passed around a bottle of supermarket wine, their laughter carrying across the square. Normal twenty-somethings doing normal twenty-something things. He wondered if any of them had brothers. If they knew where their brothers were that night.

Around him, Paris spun its usual web of café crowds lingering, tourists chasing sunset shots, buses keeping time. But above, Laslo would be readying his next canvas, choosing pigments to paint this moment of escape. Making art from the aftermath, one more time.

Nick started walking. Not toward his apartment, not toward the hotel where his mother waited, just… away. Each step put distance between himself and those paintings, between the boy he had been and the man Gene, Laslo, and all the rest had tried to make him become.

He stopped at a tabac and bought cigarettes. The man behind the counter made change without looking up. The shop's signage caught Nick's eye—hand-painted letters peeling at the edges, a typeface from the 1960s that someone in his studio would call "authentically distressed." He'd pitched something similar last week for a boutique hotel rebrand, trying to capture that same worn elegance. Now, the irony wasn't lost on him—here he stood, authentically distressed himself, no art direction required.

He kept walking until he reached the Champs-Élysées, where luxury shops gleamed like jewelry boxes, perfect and untouchable. A father and son emerged from Ladurée, the boy cradling a mint-green box of macarons. The father, his hand rested on the boy's shoulder, guided him through the crowd—such a simple gesture that Nick had to look away. He turned down darker streets in the eighth arrondissement, where the facades grew more elegant but the sidewalks emptier.

As he walked, Nick found himself checking over his shoulder, hearing footsteps that never materialized. He felt that familiar prickle between his shoulder blades—the same sensation from childhood when Gene would watch from doorways. His pace quickened. Each shop window became a mirror to check behind him, each shadow a potential threat. He imagined Laslo somewhere in the dark, sketching: *Young Man Fleeing Through the Eighth, Oil on Canvas*. Another stolen moment, another uninvited documentation of his pain.

A red awning caught his eye: Chez André, its horseshoe bar glowing with evening light. The usual crowd lined every corner: elegant Parisians sharing wine, tourists seeking refuge, drifters nursing their drinks. The maître d' looked Nick over—his rumpled clothes, his wild eyes—but led him to a corner table without comment. Jittery, Nick positioned himself with his back to the wall, clear sightlines to both entrances. When the maître d' lingered, adjusting already-straight silverware, Nick's chest tightened with a startling thought: Had Laslo called ahead? Warned them about the unstable young man who might appear? *Get it together*, Nick whispered to himself and ordered a coffee he didn't want, just to have a reason to be there. He spread Jason's letter on the white linen-covered tabletop, the paper already soft from frequent handling.

Jason's handwriting sprawled across the page—no grid, no guidelines, just raw emotion bleeding through cheap ballpoint. It was the antithesis to everything Nick presented in his work: unplanned, unkerned, brutally honest. But there was power—a truth—in its artlessness.

"I keep trying to write this letter," Jason had scribbled. "I've started it like five times now."

Nick could picture Jason hunched over a desk in his room, crumpling up version after version, each a failed attempt at telling the truth. Had he written this final version in that fast-food place back home? Or maybe even here in Paris, sitting in Laslo's studio, trying to find the words while Laslo watched and painted and did nothing to help?

"*Monsieur*." Nick waved for the waiter. The coffee was no longer enough, just a prop in this nighttime performance of normalcy. "*Un cognac, s'il vous plaît*."

A cluster of Americans swept in on a wave of laughter. Two brothers with their girlfriends in tow, the older one pulling his brother close, both lost in some shared joke. The younger one squirmed free, grinning—such simple, untainted brotherhood. Nick's lungs seized at their thoughtless intimacy.

He looked back at the letter. "Dad bought me a car. Can you believe that? A piece of crap Hyundai…" Nick could picture the car parked in the driveway of the Missouri house. Jason's last attempt at freedom. He could see Jason sitting inside for hours, radio on, going nowhere. What had he been listening to? What had the weather been like? Nick imagined one of those humid Missouri nights when the air stuck like wet wool against your skin. And where was that car now? Would there still be cassette tapes under the seats, fast-food wrappers in the glove compartment, evidence of his brother's final months?

The cognac arrived, amber liquid catching the light like Gene's workshop windows used to catch the sunset. Nick took a long sip, letting the drink burn down his throat. Another line caught his eye: "Sometimes he sits with me when it's slow and we talk about music and books and stuff." That guy Mike at the fast-food place. Had Jason been trying to tell him something too? Had he seen in Mike someone who might understand, might help? Or had he just been another Laslo—someone who watched and sympathized but only from a safe, comfortable distance?

The American voices floated to Nick's table again. "Come on, hit the Marais with us. When are you gonna be in Paris again?" the older one insisted. His brother made a show of protest—early tour tomorrow, too tired—but coziness threaded his words. He knew he'd follow, knew his brother would wait.

Nick noticed how they'd unconsciously arranged themselves in a perfect composition: the older brother as the anchor, the younger providing movement, their girlfriends framing the scene. Even in chaos, people sought balance, visual harmony. Another sip of cognac, a fresh wave of sorrow washed over Nick.

The American brothers argued now about which club to try, their voices carrying across the bar. The older one ruffled the younger one's hair, the younger ducking and laughing. Nick watched them, feeling something twist in his chest. He and Jason had never had that easy physicality, that casual brotherhood. Even before everything went wrong, they'd moved around each other like satellites. Jason had his temper, and somehow Nick couldn't shake the thought that Gene had poisoned even the possibility of brotherly affection.

The letter quivered in his hands. "I found the Sega Genesis in a box in the basement last week. Still had Aladdin in it." Nick remembered that game, the countless hours they'd spent playing. He'd loved how the monkey would help Aladdin collect apples, how there was always some hidden treasure to find if you looked hard enough. But now he wondered—had Jason been trying to recapture something in playing that old game alone at night? Some memory of him and Nick from before? A waiter arrived with fresh glasses for the American table. "Another bottle of the Côtes du Rhône?" The older brother nodded, then turned to tease his younger brother about only drinking wine in Paris. "Wait till I tell Mom you're a wine snob now."

Nick's glass stood empty. Another appeared without him registering. The American group mapped their tomorrow: Louvre, maybe Versailles. The younger brother's voice carried across the restaurant. "The Hall of Mirrors is supposed to be incredible. They say you can see yourself from every angle. Kind of creepy, honestly."

Like Laslo's studio, Nick thought. Everything reflected, repeated, documented. Pain turned into art turned into more pain. Nick's hand tightened on his drink. The cognac burned against the ice that had settled in his chest, two temperatures at war.

The Americans' laughter reverberated in the bar long after they'd left. Nick tried to remember if he and Jason had ever laughed like that together. There must have been moments: playing video games, maybe, or that summer they built a fort in the backyard. But the memories were distant, untrustworthy, like paintings viewed in bad light.

At the bar, a man watched his son bend over a tablet, the boy fighting sleep to finish his game. The father's hand rested on his shoulder, just a small, uncomplicated touch. The boy kept playing, unflinching, unguarded. He never once tensed, never measured the steps to the door, never planned escape routes.

Nick folded the letter, then unfolded it again. The creases were starting to wear thin, like old scars. How many times had his mother done this same thing over the years? Sitting in hotel rooms around the world, taking out this letter, folding and unfolding, carrying the weight of what she'd kept from her living son. Did she read the letter when she couldn't sleep? Did she sit like this too, studying each loop of Jason's pen, hunting for warnings in every curve and slash?

And now he knew Jason had been in Paris. Right here, maybe even in this same restaurant, trying to tell Laslo what he couldn't tell anyone else. Had Jason sat at this very table? Had he ordered cognac too, trying to find courage in a glass? Had he watched other brothers laugh together and felt the same twisting in his chest that Nick felt now?

The waiter's glances grew pointed as chairs scraped back, coats rustled, bills settled. People drifted into the Paris dark, untouched by what had splintered Nick apart in Laslo's studio.

Through the window, Nick could see tourists taking photos along the streets. A man lifted a little girl onto his shoulders. She spread her arms wide, pretending to fly, trusting without a second thought that she wouldn't fall. Holding her ankles, the man kept her safe without holding her back. The crack of stacking chairs jolted Nick's spine. Around him, the restaurant shed its warmth: the waiter's practiced moves with cloth and cash, business cards flashing as suits split their bill. The father and son had vanished, a half-drunk glass of milk left on the table—its ordinary innocence another blade in Nick's chest.

Nick checked his phone to find more messages from Susan: "Please let us know you're safe," "Your mother's taken something to sleep," "We need to talk about the arrangements." Arrangements, Nick thought. Such a clean word for such a mess.

And one from Laslo that made his stomach turn: "The paintings were never meant to hurt you. They were meant to show the truth."

The truth. As if truth were something that could be captured in oil paint and canvas. As if Jason's desperate visit to Paris, his nights on Laslo's couch, his attempts to speak through art and letters and accusations, could be reduced to a gallery of beautiful suffering. Nick's hand trembled. Did Laslo know he'd be checking his phone now? The text had come through just moments ago. He glanced around the restaurant. A figure by the bar studied him intently, or was Nick imagining things? The waiter who kept passing by, did he know Laslo? Was he reporting back? Nick locked the phone, the screen fading to dark.

"*On ferme, monsieur*," the waiter said, wiping down nearby tables with increasing purpose. Nick nodded and paid his bill. The cognac had left him reeling rather than drunk.

Street cleaners roamed the pre-dawn city, their green machines spitting water over concrete. The smell caught him—wet pavement and gas—and he was back in Missouri: the Ford truck gleaming with soap, Nick's hands raw from scrubbing, the weight of Jason's gaze from his bedroom window. All those Sunday mornings of forced ritual, while above them, Jason had watched. Had he known even then, seen what Nick couldn't?

Nick walked toward the river, drawn by some invisible current, the letter pulsing in his pocket with each step. At the Pont des Arts, Italian voices tumbled across the water—a girl directed her friend's poses against the railing, their cameras flashing in the regular rhythm of tourists doing regular things. Without meaning to, Nick had pulled out Jason's letter again. "Sometimes I dream about just getting in that stupid car and driving to Connecticut. Just showing up at Aunt Julia's door. But then what would I say?"

If Jason had shown up that day—if he'd actually made that drive—what would Nick have done? Slammed the door in his brother's face? Or would he have recognized what he saw there: the same pain Nick had spent years learning to hide? He could picture it so clearly now: Jason on Julia's porch, shoulders hunched in that worn denim jacket. Would Jason's eyes have held that particular kind of fear Laslo had captured so perfectly in paint—the look of someone drowning in plain sight?

A police boat moved down the river, its searchlight sweeping the banks with accusing brightness. Nick shrank back from the railing as the beam approached, heart hammering. Laslo had called them, Nick was certain, had reported the unstable young man who had physically assaulted him in his studio. The light caught the underside of the arch and moved on, but Nick's pulse kept thumping.

When the boat was fully out of sight, Nick leaned against the bridge railing, the metal biting cold through his shirt. Another line from Jason's letter floated up: "Dad encouraged it, of course. Told everyone how concerned he was about my spiritual state, about my 'tendency toward deception.'"

Gene spun stories, created narratives, and made himself appear as a concerned father dealing with troubled sons. Even now, in death, he'd managed one final performance: beloved husband, teacher, stepfather. No mention of his real sons in the obituary. Nick wondered who had written the entry. Probably the yoga teacher wife, sitting in thunderbolt pose, choosing each word carefully to paint the picture she wanted the world to see. Nick's phone buzzed again in his pocket. Susan: "At least tell me you're not with Marc."

Ha! Nick thought. Marc isn't the one you should be worried about. But then he thought of Laslo's studio, of all those paintings, of Jason sitting on that tattered couch night after night, trying to tell his story to someone who just kept turning it into art. Maybe Susan should be worried about all of them—every adult who'd watched and done nothing, who'd turned their pain into conversation pieces, who'd chosen aesthetics over action.

Gray light crept into the sky. Soon the metro would shudder awake, bakers would pull the first loaves from their ovens, cafés would arrange their tables. Precise and practiced routines. Such a normal morning. The city would wake up, and yesterday would become just another day, just another death, just another set of revelations that changed everything and nothing. He pulled out Jason's letter again, holding it with care to avoid the worn creases. A liquid stain bloomed in the corner, fresh from the restaurant. The paper had turned delicate as moth wings, each fold threatening to erase Jason's voice forever.

The Italian girls gave up on their selfie and were now asking a Japanese couple to take their picture. Everyone smiling, everyone accommodating. The kind of human interaction that happened a million times a day on this bridge. Nick watched them arrange themselves against the railing, adjust their hair, their scarves, their smiles. Making sure everything looked perfect in the frame.

Just like Gene had done. Arranging everything to look right from the outside. The good Christian father, concerned about his sons' spiritual welfare. The dedicated auto mechanic who volunteered at church. The man who bought his troubled son a car instead of asking what troubled him. Who sent his other son away—the one who flinched at every touch—instead of taking responsibility. Nick understood this kind of manipulation now—sleight of hand was part his job, part of making things beautiful. "Every design is a deception," his creative director liked to say. "We're selling what doesn't exist yet." At least Nick admitted what he was doing, while Gene's greatest design project had been concealing what he truly was. Susan's messages glowed on Nick's phone. Should he text that he was safe? But what did "safe" even mean? Neither he nor Jason had been safe since they were children, since Gene had called them to the workshop. They'd just found different ways to pretend, different places to hide.

Nick thought of Laslo's paintings again—all those captured moments no one wanted to see. Jason desperate in Paris. Nick hiding behind spreadsheets and tailored suits. Both trying to escape the same shadows, the same hands that weaponized touch. "But then what would I say?" Jason had written about showing up at Julia's. What could anyone say about the things Gene had done, about the silence that protected him, about pain documented but not prevented?

The Seine caught fire with sunrise, black water turning molten. In her hotel bed, Lynne would be waking as the pills wore off. While in Missouri, practiced hands were positioning Gene's body just so, preparing his last deception.

Nick pulled away from the railing. He tucked the letter back in his pocket, Jason's words pulsating against his heart like a bruise.

Where now? His apartment with its echoes of Laslo? The hotel where his mother waited with shaky explanations? Or somewhere new—another city, another life, another way to pretend the past couldn't follow?

Paris sparkled in the morning light, beautiful and indifferent to everything: the weight of memory, the stories trapped in paint, the truths that had come too late.

Three

1.

The air inside Nick's bedroom clung to him, as if the walls had absorbed the stillness of the night. Shadows pooled in the corners, stretching long and heavy, untouched by the faint light seeping through the curtains. The faint, lingering smell of something metallic mingled with the dull musk of undisturbed furniture. The oppressive quiet swallowed each soft thud of his shoes. The space reverberated against him, as if the room had settled into its own emptiness. The silence weighed on his ears, made him acutely aware of the heft of his own breath. His legs ached from hours of wandering the streets, from standing on the Pont des Arts, from everything that had happened with Laslo. The desperate grabbing echoed from another lifetime. The wrinkled, moist letter rested against his pocket.

His bed remained untouched, the sheets pulled tight with hospital corners his mother had drilled into him—just one of many ways she imposed order in chaos. She had insisted on discipline in the smallest of tasks, as if precision in folding fabric could hold back the unpredictable currents of life. He could still hear her voice correcting him, still feel the ghost of her hands smoothing out imperfections.

The room smelled of stale air and the remnants of last night, the mingling scents of coffee and liquor clinging to his clothes. The sharp bite of cognac from the bar, the yeasty warmth of morning bread from the brasserie below—the effect was something almost tangible, something that wrapped around him like the weight of the past. Too many smells, too many memories, too many hours without sleep. The night had stretched long and merciless, slipping into morning without his realization. His body ached with exhaustion, his mind dull from obsessive thinking and too little rest. And still, the day waited for him, indifferent.

The door rattled under someone's knuckles.

"Nick?" Susan's voice. "I know you're in there. I saw your light from the street."

He put his forehead against the cool wall beside the door. His whole body dragged with exhaustion, each movement slow, like pushing through water. When had he last slept? Before Gene died? Before he'd seen Laslo's paintings? He couldn't remember.

She knocked again. "We need to talk about the funeral arrangements."

The word "arrangements" reverberated like a sounding gong in his exhausted brain. Everything being arranged, always being arranged. His whole life had been one long arrangement.

When he opened the door, Susan's small frame tensed even smaller, shoulders knotted. She wore different clothes from yesterday, but fatigue had sculpted rivets under her eyes. Join the club, Nick thought.

"Nick—" Susan strode past him into the apartment. "Your mother's still sleeping. Like I said, the hotel doctor gave her something." She paused in the center of the room, looking lost in the grey morning light. "They want us in Missouri by tomorrow night. I don't know if we'll go."

Nick said nothing, just leaned against the wall. Unsaid things crowded the room.

"I keep thinking about when it happened," Susan said finally, her professor's posture crumbling. Her hands twisted together, a gesture he'd never seen from her before. "When you were sent away. I remember, Nick. I watched it happen." Her voice grew tight with old regret. "Gene would say things about how you were taking advantage of Jason, and he'd talk about fresh starts and healing through separation. He was so subtle—just dropping thoughts into conversation like pebbles into a pond. Never explaining anything, but always making you out to sound monstrous. And Lynne, she was drowning in guilt and confusion. By the time she announced her decision to send you to Julia's, she truly believed it was her own idea. I didn't see it then, but now..." She stopped, pressed her hand to her mouth.

Nick's vision swam. How long had he been awake? Twenty-four hours? More? Through the fog of weariness, a thought seeped in like poison: Had Gene wanted Nick gone because he had finally started fighting back that last year—locking his bedroom door, screaming when Gene came near? His body remembered before his mind did, the instinct kicking in—to shrink, to brace against the wall like he once did against his bedroom door.

Morning light crept through the windows, dust motes swirling gold, while below, the brasserie stirred to life, the scent of coffee and fresh croissants rising with the hum of breakfast service. But to Nick, in this moment of dizzying revelation, the smells and sounds of normalcy rang obscene. Nick tried to let Susan do the talking. Tried not to interrupt or say a word, even biting his tongue and holding it in place. He bit—not its tip, but its midsection—a large, domineering bite that might have hurt had he paid it any mind. And yet, he so wanted to interrupt her, to interrupt her the way one does when they know they are about to intrude and shock someone with a word that is at once exquisite, reckless, and obscene.

Laslo's neck still burned against his palms. The cognac coated his tongue. Reality wavered at the edges, as if he were watching someone else's movie unfold.

"I'm not going to the funeral," Nick said at last. He propped against the open door, his escape route ready. The words rang with finality—of course he wouldn't go, had never considered going—and the certainty steadied him.

"No," Susan said. "I didn't think you would." She moved toward an armchair near the window, then stopped, remembering something. "Can I sit?"

"You've been here before." Nick closed the door, his temples pounding with each heartbeat.

"Yes, but..." Susan's hand drifted in the air between them. "After last night, everything feels different." She sat, her bag clutched in her lap like a shield. "Your mother wants to go. She says she has to. For appearances."

"Appearances," Nick repeated. The letter burned in his pocket, heavier with each passing hour. "Like when she sent me to Aunt Julia's? For appearances?"

The room tilted. Days had blurred past food. The cognac churned in his empty stomach.

"Nick—"

"Or when she let Jason go off to that college? That was for appearances too, wasn't it?"

"It's not that simple." Susan's tone edged with something hard.

"Isn't it?" Nick remained standing, his back against the door. He needed its solidity to stay upright. "Seems pretty simple to me. Keep up appearances. Hide the truth. Ship your kids off when they start asking questions."

Susan opened her mouth to respond, the shape of her words forming in the space between them, but another knock interrupted, sharp and deliberate. The sound rippled through the room, and her jaw tightened as her gaze shifted to the door. They both stopped, still as if caught in the knock's reverberation, the air thick with the weight of the unexpected. Even the soft hum of the radiator grew distant now, overtaken by the moment's unease.

"Nick?" Lynne's voice, thick with whatever sedatives she had taken. At least one of them had slept. "Nick, my boy, are you awake?"

Susan's face went pale. "I didn't know she'd—"

"Nick?" Lynne knocked again, harder. Each beat landed directly on Nick's temples. "I can hear voices. Susan? Are you in there?"

Morning invaded through the floorboards—chairs scraping, orders shouted, a coffee machine's iron throat clearing. Exhaustion twisted these everyday sounds like reflections in funhouse mirrors, familiar images warping menacingly.

Nick looked at Susan, who hadn't moved from the armchair. "Should I—"

Susan's voice carried the weight of truth: "You have to let her in. You know you do."

"Nick?" Another knock. "Please."

He opened the door. Lynne stood there in the same clothes from last night, her perfect makeup at last cracked, showing the person beneath. The hallway light caught the silver in her hair. When had that happened? When had his mother gotten old?

"I couldn't sleep," she said, pushing past him into the apartment. She stopped when she saw Susan. "Oh."

The walls moved closer, shrinking the room to a trap. Three people, three truths. Pain hammered Nick's skull with each heartbeat.

"The doctor gave you something," Susan said to Lynne. "You should be resting."

"How could I rest?" Lynne's voice had a wild edge. "When my son is…" She turned to Nick. "When both my sons are…"

The morning light poured in now, sharp and unrelenting, exposing everything they might have wished to hide: Fine lines etched into Lynne's face, turning her weariness into something brittle and raw. Dark circles bloomed beneath Susan's eyes, remnants of too many sleepless nights and not enough answers. Nick leaned harder against the door, his shoulders locked in a futile attempt to anchor himself. Every joint, every muscle weighted, as if the universe had conspired overnight to pull him down. The room blazed like an over-lit stage, hot and exposing, leaving no place for them to retreat.

"I went to Laslo's studio," Nick said. The words dropped into the room like stones into still water. He swallowed against the waxy taste coating his tongue.

"What do you mean?" Lynne sank onto the couch. "What does Laslo have to do with any of this?"

"He has paintings," Nick said, his tired voice strange in his own ears. "Hundreds of them. Of us. Of everything."

Susan made a small sound, and something broke in her throat. "Nick—"

"He painted Jason in his studio. Here in Paris. When Jason came to visit." Nick watched his mother's face, his vision blurring at the edges. "But you knew about that visit, didn't you? Both of you knew."

Steam hissed through the pipes in the walls. Nick could feel the vibrations in his bones, in his teeth, in the growing headache behind his eyes.

"We thought—" Susan started, but Lynne cut her off.

"We thought it would be better if you didn't know. You were doing so well at the bank. Building your own life here. Jason was... He was so angry. So confused. We thought seeing each other might make things worse for both of you."

"Worse?" Nick laughed in such a way that it hurt his throat. "Worse than what happened? Worse than him hanging himself in his dorm room?"

The morning light turned the dust motes swirling between them into golden snow, and they fell softly in the terrible silence that followed his words. Nick watched them drift, mesmerized, and he saw his mother's hands move to and fro, smoothing imaginary wrinkles in her clothing. He'd seen the gesture thousands of times: always tidying, always trying to make things appear neat and orderly. Even now, with everything lying in pieces around them, she still wanted to smooth things over. And Susan, perched in his armchair like she sat at attention during a faculty meeting, her reasonable voice ready to explain everything, to contextualize, to make sense of what could never make sense. The room swam every time Nick looked at her.

Something shifted in Nick then, like a key turning in a lock. Or maybe exhaustion had won out. There was no point in talking to them, he realized. They would keep talking in circles, keep offering explanations and justifications, keep trying to reshape the past into something manageable. But Jason was still dead. Gene was dead. And all the words in the world couldn't change that.

He moved away from the door at last and went to his kitchen counter to start making coffee. The familiar routine of choosing a coffee pod, filling the water tank, letting the machine wheeze to life slowly stilled his shaking hands.

"Nick?" His mother's voice called, uncertain. "What are you doing?"

"Making coffee," he said. The words stuck like syrup in his mouth, slow and cloying. His tongue felt swollen with too many hours awake, too many drinks, too many truths poured out like liquor in the dark. "You're going to need it."

"Why would we…?" Susan ventured.

"Because you're leaving."

He thrust two tiny espresso cups in their direction, not caring if the coffee spilled. Hot liquid splashed over the rims, stained dark his mother's shirt sleeve.

"Drink up and get out."

They left without arguing. Maybe they saw something in his face—some reflection of Gene's anger, or Jason's desperation, or just the raw fatigue that made his hands shake and his vision blur. The door clicked shut behind them, leaving him alone in the quiet apartment.

Nick stood there, swaying. The harsh light burned his eyes. His bed remained made. He didn't bother undressing. Didn't bother pulling back the blankets. Just fell onto the mattress, Jason's letter crinkling in his pocket. Before his eyes closed, he watched more dust motes dance in the light, like gilded snow, like ashes, like the pieces of his life that would never fit together again. Sleep swept over him like a wave, dragging him under into darkness where he found no paintings, no letters, no gentle hands or cruel ones. Just blessed nothing stretching outward like the Seine at dawn, endless and empty and clean.

2.

Susan's fingers jerked and spasmed, each movement betraying the restless energy surging through her. Her pulse hammered in her ears, relentless and sharp, like the echo of a distant drum. She flexed her hands in a futile attempt to steady them, but the espresso Nick had forced on them earlier coursed through her veins. Every amplified heartbeat threatened to crack open her chest. She hated espresso—had always hated it—but the wild mix of exasperation and irritation in Nick's eyes, winter blue in the harsh light, had made refusal impossible.

The hotel room around her felt both claustrophobic and too large. The maid had come earlier, tidying with precision: smoothing the bed until every wrinkle vanished, collecting the empty bottles, wiping down the surfaces. Yet the scent of cigarette smoke still lingered, mixed with the faint tang of spilled wine and something heavier. Grief, maybe. It clung to the air, to her skin, as if woven into the fabric of the place.

She swayed, her hand skimming the wall for balance, her knees faltering under too much weight. Gripping the edge of the sink, she bent over, her breath coming in shallow gasps. Her reflection in the mirror blurred as nausea clawed its way upward. She reached the toilet just as the bile rose, violent and unrelenting. The retching echoed off the marble tiles, sharp and metallic, making her wince. Even the hotel towels, soft and thick, scraped against her clammy skin like sandpaper as she wiped her face.

Through the open bathroom door, she could see Lynne silhouetted against the window, bordered by the gray morning light. Lynne hadn't moved since they returned to the room, her thin frame stiff and unyielding as she stared down at the street below. Her wrinkled silk blouse, the same one she'd worn yesterday, hung on her body like it belonged to someone else. Susan's stomach twisted again, but this time coffee wasn't the culprit.

She forced herself to move to the desk, though each step made her head spin. Their travel documents lay scattered across the polished wood—passports, plane tickets, hotel confirmations. Susan began sorting them, placing each piece in its designated spot. This ritual of organizing had always soothed and given her a sense of control in the chaos of their lives. She and Lynne were the same in this way. But today, the papers felt weightless, meaningless, like artifacts from a life she barely recognized.

Her gaze fell on the South African Airways tickets. Business class, of course. Lynne always insisted on business class, even when they couldn't afford it. Susan's hands hovered over the seating assignments, double-checking the numbers again and again as a strange fear gripped her. What if they were separated during the flight? As if sitting together could somehow hold everything else together.

The room tilted as her jittery body fought against the excess caffeine. Susan grabbed her passport and flipped open the pages, needing something solid to ground her. She opened to the emergency contact section, and her pen hovered over the blank line. Lynne's name should go there, of course. They'd been together for fifteen years. But as Susan glanced at Lynne, still standing by the window, something stopped her. Could she really put Lynne's name? After everything? After all the secrets about Gene, about Jason? A deep unease settled in her chest, heavier than the coffee—induced anxiety. Nick's name appeared on the line even before she'd decided to write it. The letters appeared final, irreversible, staring back at her in sharp blue ink. If something did happen—if their plane went down somewhere over Africa—would he even care? Would he want to be notified?

A wave of dizziness hit her, and she set the passport down, retreating again to the bathroom. The clock on the desk showed ten-thirty. The morning wore on endlessly, stretching and folding in on itself like a cruel trick of time. She grabbed the thick white hotel robes hanging on the bathroom door and walked back into the room.

"Here," she said, tossing one toward Lynne. The robe landed in a crumpled heap at her feet, a soft white puddle against the worn carpet. Lynne didn't move, didn't even flinch. Her breath fogged the glass in front of her, a faint halo spreading outward from her reflection.

Susan leaned against the desk, watching Lynne's back. The sharp lines of Lynne's shoulder blades stood out against the fabric of her blouse, stark and fragile, like wings trying to break free. Minutes passed. With movements so slow they felt dreamlike, Lynne began to undress. Each piece of clothing fell to the floor with a muted rustle: jacket, blouse, skirt. She stood in her undergarments for a moment, goosebumps rising on her bare arms, before slipping the robe on and tying a loose knot at the waist.

Lynne headed straight for the minibar. Of course, she would choose the minibar. Susan leaned against the desk, arms crossed, watching as Lynne yanked open the small fridge and rummaged through its contents. Glass clinked against glass, a discordant melody of indecision. Lynne's fingers hesitated for a moment before closing around a tiny bottle of Grey Goose. She pulled the bottle out, turning it in her hand, the shiny blue cap flashing under the dim hotel light. Without a glance at Susan, she twisted the top off with a practiced motion, the quiet pop cutting through the silence between them.

"What are we going to do?" Lynne's voice carried across the room. She stood with the minibar door still open, cold air pooling around her ankles. The vodka dangled from her fingers like a lifeline.

"For starters, close the damn refrigerator," Susan snapped. The words came out harsher than she intended. The caffeine had made her cruel. She strode across the room and slammed the door shut, the force of it rattling all the tiny bottles of liquor. Startling them both, the sound had broken the fragile tension in the air.

Lynne unscrewed the vodka and took a long sip. Susan watched Lynne's throat work as she swallowed, the movement curious and hypnotic. Fifteen years together, and Lynne could still catch her off guard. The elegant line of her neck, the vulnerability in her hands, the way she tried so hard to hold herself together even as everything else fell apart.

The first sob slipped out, nothing more than a breath. Lynne's face twisted, her features collapsing inward as if something deep inside her had given way. Then the flood came. Tears spilled down her cheeks in heavy, relentless waves, black streaks of mascara running like dark paths through her pale skin. She sucked in a shaky breath which caught in her throat, breaking into a sharp, involuntary gasp. Her hands flew to her mouth, fingers digging into her cheeks as if she could package the grief back inside, keep it from spilling out any further. But the sobs, breaking past her hands, escaped in choked, guttural sounds—raw, unfiltered, impossible to suppress.

Her whole body shook, wracked with the force of devastation. She doubled over and pulled her elbows tight against her ribs. The weight of everything she had held back for so long now crushed down on her. She tried to slow her breathing, to find some rhythm, but each time she thought she had steadied, another sob tore through her, violent and unrelenting. The sheer helplessness of it all clawed at her, the grief blunt and merciless, offering no relief, no space to catch her breath.

"What is it?" Susan asked, though the question felt naive the moment it left her lips. Of course, she already knew. The answer had never changed. She steeled herself for the familiar lament—the guilt, the failures, the endless self-recriminations that spilled from Lynne like a broken record.

Susan knew this routine: the same apologies, the same regrets, circling back on themselves, never leading anywhere. She had rehearsed her responses so many times they came out like lines from a play, her voice measured, her words chosen to soothe without inviting more. She knew that nothing she said would matter. They had repeated this ritual too many times to count, each performance just as exhausting as the last.

But this time, Lynne said something different.

"My husband is dead."

The words tore from Lynne's throat, primal and shattering in their simplicity. Susan froze, the room tilting around her as the weight of those four words settled in. A kaleidoscope of emotions spun through her: jealousy, pity, disgust, love. How many nights had she listened to Lynne's stories about Gene—about his cruelty, his manipulation, his coldness? She had built up such a store of hatred for a man she'd only known in a detached way, a shadow that had haunted their relationship from the start. And yet. Here Lynne sat, her Lynne, sobbing for *him*. Mourning *him*. Still caught in the web he'd spun around her heart all those years ago. Slowly, as though her body weighed twice as much as it should, Lynne shuffled toward the bed and sank onto the edge, her shoulders heaving.

Susan crossed the room with measured steps, the weight of her own anger and confusion fading in the face of Lynne's unraveling. Whatever resentment had simmered beneath the surface now grew small and insignificant against the raw grief spilling out in front of her. Without hesitation, Susan lowered herself onto the bed beside Lynne and pulled her in, wrapping her arms around her.

Lynne collapsed into the embrace, her body shaking as sobs ripped through her with a force that made Susan tighten her hold. The deep, gut-wrenching cries made Susan's chest ache. Not just sadness, but something buried, something unspoken, broke free in ragged gasps. Susan rested her chin against Lynne's head, felt Lynne's shaking breaths rise and fall, watched as her fingers clutched at Susan's sleeve. No words could fix this type of loss. No reassurances could soften the pain. So Susan held her wife and let the storm pass through them both.

They stayed like that as the morning aged around them, the sun climbing higher in the sky. Lynne's tears soaked into Susan's robe, her breath coming in uneven gasps. The smell of cigarette smoke and fresh grief lingered in the air, heavy and unyielding. Somewhere across Paris, Nick slept, oblivious to the unraveling happening in their tiny hotel room. And somewhere in Missouri, Gene's body waited for whatever came next.

3.

The light filtering through Nick's blinds cast a disjointed pattern on the floor, like water seeping from a leaky faucet. Nick lay in bed, a headache pulsing behind his eyes in time with his heartbeat. The walls seemed to breathe, expanding and contracting around him, while stale air hung motionless. He couldn't remember if he had just woken up or if he had been drifting in and out of consciousness all day. Time had lost its meaning since the events of the morning.

His mother and Susan had left, just as he had wanted, but now, in the quiet of the apartment, regret and uncertainty took over. The crumpled letter held the truth that he couldn't bear to read again. Jason's words had left behind a residue of anger and disappointment that seeped into every part of Nick.

Stumbling to the bathroom, Nick was unprepared for the disjointed reflection staring back at him in the mirror. He looked worse than he felt, a mess of hair and vapid eyes betraying the turmoil inside him. He splashed cold water on his face, an attempt at bringing clarity that in reality only intensified the chill spreading through his chest.

Showering morphed into a routine motion, his movements robotic and detached. He stood under the scalding water, hoping to wash away the pain and confusion inside him. But when he emerged, nothing had changed.

His reflection in the steamed mirror looked like a stranger's. Twenty-eight years old, standing in his Paris apartment, and somehow he felt twelve again, powerless, confused. Gene's death should have freed him—isn't that what people said about outliving their abusers? Instead, he felt trapped in a maze of contradictions. Part of him wanted to fly to Missouri, to see the body, to make sure Gene really had died. Another part wanted to pretend he'd never received the news, to go about his day as if nothing had changed.

The worst part was its mundanity—a heart attack, in his sleep. Such an ordinary death for a man who'd caused such extraordinary damage. No dramatic confrontation, no chance for Nick to show Gene that he'd survived without him. His expensive turtleneck, his Paris apartment, his carefully curated existence—these were proof that Nick had built a life despite everything, evidence that Gene would now never see. All Nick was left with was an obituary that didn't even mention him or Jason and a hollow feeling that mixed relief and rage.

And then came the fear—a gnawing, insidious thing that crept in alongside the anger. Unbidden, his thoughts turned to Gene's stepdaughters, the innocent bystanders in Gene's latest facade of familial bliss. What had they endured? Nick's stomach churned at the possibility of their suffering, the unknown horrors that might have unfolded behind closed doors.

Gene could twist even the most hurtful actions into gestures of love, his manipulations carefully veiled as concern. Had he done the same to them? The thought sent a shudder through Nick's body. It had been one thing to endure Gene's warped affections himself, but the possibility of those young girls…

"Please, no." Nick squeezed his eyes shut against the sudden onslaught of images—innocent faces marred by unseen scars. Had he been too preoccupied with his own terrible memories to consider them? To protect them? Was he complicit through his silence, his absence? He couldn't stay here, couldn't sit with these thoughts, with the realization that he'd spent years arranging his life around a man who could now be reduced to a death notice, a funeral arrangement, an empty space where all his unresolved questions used to live.

Dressed in simple, dark clothes, Nick left the apartment and vanished into the night. The city's chaos and anonymity offered a fleeting solace, a temporary escape from the weight pressing down on him. But deep down, he knew—no matter how far or fast he ran, he couldn't outrun his own conflicted feelings. He had no destination, but what did it matter? All that mattered was movement, the desperate need to keep going, to outrun whatever was clawing its way up inside him.

4.

The shadow fell across Nick's table before he saw the man.

Ice flooded Nick's veins. His shoulders hunched forward, ribs suddenly too tight around his lungs. For a moment, Nick was thirteen years old again, frozen in place as a familiar silhouette filled the doorway. Gene's shadow had moved just like this, slow and deliberate, knowing there was nowhere for Nick to run.

Nick's fingers tightened around his tepid tequila, the ice long melted, leaving only the ghost of cold. The condensation made the glass slippery, and the drink threatened to slide from his grip. He forced himself to breathe, to remember where he was—a dingy bar with disco balls and pulsing music. He'd never thought much about coming to such a place, though he couldn't quite explain why. The space had transformed as night deepened, held both possibility and resignation in equal measure.

The shadow man's scent was behind him now—a thick and musky cologne. Nick's phone pulsed against his thigh, and Nick felt thankful for something to focus on besides his skin prickling with remembered dread.

"Anything interesting?"

"No," Nick said, not looking up. The word came out sharper than intended, a reflexive defense. He'd chosen this spot specifically to observe without being observed: close enough to the streetlamp's glow through the window to see but far enough from the dance floor to think. The early evening crowd had filtered in for the past hour—the bartender with geometric tattoos who never seemed to smile, the elderly queen holding court in her corner booth, the too-eager students trying to look worldly. He'd been watching them all, letting their small mysteries distract him from what had driven him here in the first place. *Time of death. Cause of death.*

The shadow shifted, and at last Nick looked up. The man stood half-hidden in the bar's terrible lighting, but his presence filled the space around them. Bald head, full beard, hairs that twirled at the edges. Nick moved his eyes over the man's skinny jeans and crisp white V-neck, the latter displaying a chest that came from dedication, not genetics. Nothing like Gene's soft, spreading middle and thinning hair. This man had the controlled grace of a jaguar, every gesture deliberate but not threatening. Not yet.

"Oh. It's you."

The words tumbled out as Nick's brain caught up with what his body already knew—this wasn't Gene.

"It's me." Though the shadow man stood almost hidden by the dark bar lighting, his voice reverberated above the trendy electronic beats.

It's me. The words tossed into the air as if their meaning were self-evident, as if the two already knew each other. Noticing Nick's hesitation, the shadow man had decided to cut through the pretense. A reminder rather than an introduction. From someone else, *It's me* might have been laced with irony, a deliberate provocation, something meant to disarm or amuse—the verbal equivalent of an old gentleman tipping his hat with just a bit too much flair—but landing somewhere between charm and self-conscious performance. From someone more reserved, the words might have been careful, tentative—spoken with caution and fragility. But here, from the shadow man, *It's me* was neither forceful nor expectant. His words were casual, inevitable, a coin tossed into a well—no splash, no echo, just the predictable motion of something long ingrained. And perhaps too a subtle jab at the awkward mechanics of encounters like these at bars like this, where introductions always teetered between formality and tension.

The man gestured toward the beat-up faux leather seat beside Nick, and when he sat, he spread his legs wide in that unconscious way confident men occupy space. But he kept his hands visible, resting on his own thighs, and Nick was thankful for the room to breathe. The perfunctory gesture passed between them, something to be acknowledged and then discarded, now as good a time as any, given that they were apart from the thick of the room, where bodies swayed and pulsed in the deepening rhythm of the night.

The music shifted overhead, bass guitar and heavy snare drum drowning out whatever remix had been playing before. Orange light flooded the room, harsh and unforgiving, and Nick could see the man clearly now—hazel eyes held steady on Nick. When he did speak, Nick experienced all these sensations, the timbre of his voice, the uncertainty of observing his body.

"Are you happy?"

The question hit Nick like cold water. His hand flew up instinctively, shielding himself from those ember-bright eyes. What kind of opening line was that? But something in the man's tone—curious rather than predatory—kept Nick from bolting.

The man spoke again. "Like what you see?"

This was more familiar territory, the usual bar banter. Nick's mouth opened, closed, opened again. He nodded, unable to form words, and that's when the man's hand landed on Nick's thigh. Heat gathered beneath Nick's trousers, sweat threatening to break through.

"Don't be afraid." The man reached over the width of Nick's chest and pulled Nick into an embrace. For a moment, Nick recoiled, his body moist not just from the sweltering room but now from this stranger's unexpected intimacy. The man clamped his free hand on Nick's shoulder and whispered, "I won't hurt you." He withdrew and returned to his power stance.

The words were surely meant to be seductive, but they hit something deeper in Nick. Gene had never said that. Gene had never bothered with reassurances.

"I'm Carlos."

The words bounced off Nick's ears and failed to penetrate his thoughts. He had returned to the gravity of the news. Died in his sleep, no pain. Funeral arrangements. Laslo's fucking paintings. Stammering something about needing the restroom, Nick fled, leaving Carlos at the cramped booth with his legs spread and his hands empty.

In the bathroom, Nick ran scalding water over his fingers until they turned red and tried to wash away the phantom feeling of other hands, other times. The attendant offered him a hand towel and a spritz of cheap cologne, but Nick barely heard over the voices in his head—Gene's voice mixing with Lynne's, Laslo's paintings, and all the things that needed to be sorted.

Back on the bar floor, Nick stopped short of the table and watched as the shadow man fiddled with something, his phone most likely. And now Nick saw the object light up, watched the man raise it to his ear. Nick took a step forward. He did not need to strain to listen. The man's words carried across the bar, his voice nearer and louder than any background noise.

"Hey, it's me. I'm in a bar. Just checking in to make sure everything's okay?"

There was a short back and forth, a small exchange. Only when the man had hung up the phone did Nick return to this seat.

"Oh, there you are," the man said. "Thought you'd run off." He stuck out his hand with oddly formal politeness. "I'm Carlos," he repeated.

The look on the man's face—a questioning look, a cross between "What's with you?" and "Why don't you tell me your name?"—played at something assuring in Nick. "I'm Carlos." The words were a reprieve, like a cold ice pack on a hot forehead. When Nick heard the name the second time, heard and processed it, "I'm Carlos" became a balm: candy offered to a child who's about to throw a tantrum, a sweet to coax a child into not losing his shit. There were the feelings before "I'm Carlos" and the feelings after. Momentarily, Nick's anxiety filed itself away in the recesses of his mind, his hesitation replaced by the cool serenity of Carlos's name.

And to shut out Gene's voice in his head, the weight of shadows in doorways, Nick decided to stop running from this particular ghost. He took Carlos's hand—warm, alive, present.

"Nick."

"The rain is something, isn't it, Nick?" Carlos said. "Hard and fast, suddenly."

Nick, looking out toward the front of the bar, straining to see past the howl of dancing fools and awkward lovers, could make out the blurred red and green of traffic lights and the shrinking queue of customers at an outdoor food stall opposite.

Carlos lit a cigarette, offered Nick a drag, and touched his thigh again, gently this time. "I sort of like the atmosphere, though."

The aggression from before had evaporated. What remained was just as masculine but somehow softer, like Carlos wanted to transpose the earlier energy, or like he sensed that Nick was carrying more than just the usual baggage people brought to places like this.

"So you're new here?" Nick swallowed some of his drink to moisten his mouth. He immediately regretted his choice of words. This made Nick sound like a regular and not here because of the—

"Been here once or twice. I meant the rain."

Nick shivered and at once began to imagine flash flooding, as if the whole city could wash away. He had come here tonight to seek distraction, to drown the truth he had been suppressing for hours. But the rainy night, the presence of this mysterious man—Nick grappled to remember his role.

Carlos stood. "Nick, what will you have?"

"Oh, tequila. On the rocks."

Carlos went to the bar, and despite an almost irrational wish to escape, Nick didn't move away. He let his focus slip past Carlos, his gaze drifting to some vague point in the distance—just enough to create a pause, a momentary absence. He did not want to ignore Carlos, not exactly, but to pull back just enough to test whether Carlos would notice. Would he feel the shift, try to close the gap? Nick wanted Carlos to wonder what had changed, to sense that something, however small, had been withheld.

Nick's fingers tightened around the glass in his hand, as if that could hold back the thoughts steamrolling ahead, reckless and insistent. He pretended to be detached, but the act itself was anything but. In fact, Nick's feigned nonchalance made his intent all the more obvious. A man trying too hard to appear indifferent isn't indifferent at all.

Nick realized then that he had not been out, alone or with friends, for many months, perhaps even a year or more. It was, he told himself, because of work and the stress of being in a new job. But this account for his self-described drought did not hold. There was the money, or lack thereof, for one thing. But something else had shifted in the preceding months. Something he couldn't quite identify, something with a deep, fated connection to his father's death.

"Did you say a shot or on the rocks?" Carlos had returned, a single shot glass in one hand and two highballs balanced in the other.

"Oh, on the rocks, but either is fine…"

"But you said on the rocks…"

"I did."

"Well, I couldn't be sure, so I took both."

Déjà vu. The same still versus sparkling water scene unfolding again. The gesture should have come off as thoughtful, maybe even a little neurotic, buying two variations of tequila. But Nick could not bring himself into a mood of sentimentality. He grabbed the shot glass and poured the vodka into the tumbler, which he downed without hesitation.

On another night, in another mood, Nick might have seen Carlos's double-drink dilemma in a different light: a nervous habit, the reflex of someone eager to please. In short, Carlos trying to make a good impression—or maybe showing off. *I'm Carlos; I can buy you two top-shelf drinks.*

"So you forgive me?"

Nick sighed, his voice laced with just enough edge to suggest that, if it were up to him, he'd rather not play games.

Carlos kept talking. "I'm acting weird, I know, I'm sorry. Actually, I had one earlier, and maybe I'm already tipsy, and—"

Looking around the room, Carlos was searching for the next thing to say to fill the silence, or to give Nick space to interrupt. Nick heard the rain beat down against the skylights harder and became aware, at last, of his silence, and he imagined that his silence might be the cause of Carlos's shift in demeanor.

"You did nothing wrong." Now, Nick could be the cool one, saying suave things, speaking words ahead of their time. But the earnest smile his words brought to Carlos's face frightened Nick. He knew that people could bolt out of your life almost as soon as they appeared. Sometimes you wanted them to go, as he had once wanted his father to disappear and as he had wanted Susan and Lynne to vacate his apartment, but sometimes you yearned for the other to stay, begged them not to leave, threw yourself at them like a sick person in need of some cure only they could provide. And Nick had slowly realized, in this loud bar sequestered from the grim Paris night, that Carlos could maybe, even if impossibly, be the latter.

He looked at Carlos, hoping to study the man in more detail. With the light now a gentle pink, Nick could take in Carlos's features for certain: how his nose lay a little too flat on his angular jawline, and how his eyes settled into some indescribable hue—not really hazel, but flecked with amber and something darker, a fire just before cooling to ash. Nick knew this face, and he wanted to say so, but Carlos spoke first:

"You look lost."

"I was going to say that you look familiar."

"We've met before?"

"No, you just have this look of… well, I don't know, can't describe it."

Nick almost said that Carlos had the kind of look that puts you at ease—comforting, familiar. He carried himself with an effortless cool, the kind of guy who could hold your attention for an hour, maybe a whole night. But Nick held back, reminding himself that he wanted Carlos to be more than just a passing thought—he wanted him to be a distraction, however long that might last.

"Most people look familiar in a place like this."

"Do they? I don't come here often."

"It's not just in this particular club," Carlos said, pointing to a twenty-something at the bar who was deep in conversation with a much older man. The older man leaned against the counter while the younger moved in a curious two-step around him, acting out his words.

"The young one looks familiar. I might even have slept with him, or someone very similar looking to him. They're all interchangeable anyway, the young ones."

"Do you do that often? Sleep with younger men?" Nick lifted his tequila glass to his mouth and waited, scared to hear the answer.

Carlos's smile turned sheepish. One-timers, he said he called them. The blond one-timer, the brunette one-timer, and the unfortunate ginger one-timer.

"Sorry," Carlos said, "This isn't polite conversation." He leaned in and gestured toward the bar. "Though considering the bartender just stripped off his shirt, I don't think anyone is here for polite chit chat."

But Nick had chosen this bar *because* of what it was: a dingy place where people came to get blackout drunk and have meaningless hookups. The kind of place where you'd wake up the next morning with a splitting headache and hazy memories of going home with a stranger. Outside, the rain continued to pour its relentless tap-tap-tap, a hypnotic sound that left everything feeling inevitable. Nick glared at Carlos, now very white in the ever-changing light, then looked away. The crowd blurred together, faces becoming interchangeable, and Nick let himself drift backward. It had been raining that night too.

5.

The workshop was always cold. The perpetual chill seeped into Nick's bones long before anything else. At thirteen years old, he was small for his age, trying to make himself smaller still.

Gene moved without worry in the workshop. Gone was the loud, aggressive persona he displayed around Lynne or with his clients or at church. Instead, he was calculated. Predatory—a false gentleness always worse than anger. Anger is at least honest.

"You're my son," Gene would say, his hand already reaching out, the words a ritual more than a comfort. "This is how fathers show love."

Nick learned early on that love could be a weapon. A thing to be twisted, manipulated, used to confuse and control. Gene's abuse had never been just physical—it had been a comprehensive assault on understanding, on trust, on the very concept of familial connection.

After? The most dangerous time. When Gene attempted to reconstruct the moment, to reframe violation as affection. He'd bring Nick a glass of chocolate milk, ruffle his hair, speak in soft tones that contradicted everything he'd committed. As if tenderness could erase trauma. As if love could be administered like a medicinal dose, healing wounds by pure force of parental will.

"You're special," Gene would say in a sweet voice. "Only special sons get this kind of attention."

Each gesture of supposed love was a lie. Each soft touch a continuation of the violation. Nick learned to dissociate, to float above these moments, to become something other than himself—a ghost witnessing his own destruction.

These scenes that Nick's father had created, these machinations of sick father-son love, were not romantic nor tender.

No more than Laslo's awful paintings were. They were maps of trauma. Geographies of pain. Representations of the distance Gene had forced between Nick and any genuine understanding of love.

And now, with Carlos in this bar, Nick could test things, seeing if touch could mean something else. If a connection could be rebuilt. If a stranger's genuine interest could begin to dismantle the architecture of abuse his father had constructed.

The rain outside wasn't just rain. It was washing. Cleansing. Attempting to create space between then and now.

6.

"I'm going to take that as a no."

"Huh?" Nick snapped back to reality, Carlos's words breaking through his thoughts with a sharp crack. He had been lost in daydreams, drifting back to a time long gone, but a time that still lingered in his mind. It was a time when waiting on his father, or any man for that matter, was all too familiar. But now, he had grown and outgrown those days (or so he liked to believe). His eyes refocused on the present, taking in the dark bar and the man sitting next to him.

"I asked if you wanted another drink," Carlos repeated, his voice casual but with an edge of impatience.

"Sorry, I was lost in my thoughts… something sinister," Nick replied, shaking off the memories.

"'Sinister'? Who are you, man? No one here uses words like that."

That's because I don't belong here, Nick thought to himself.

But something in Carlos's gentle ribbing made Nick's chest tighten with an unexpected snugness. Nobody had seen him, seen past his deliberate words and distant manner, in a long time. Even this small moment of being called out was like a window opening in a stuffy room. Nick found himself fighting a smile, wondering if maybe, just maybe, he had found a place where his differences might be understood rather than tolerated.

"Another tequila?" Nick asked, motioning to the bartender. "I'll buy this round."

"No need. I've got it covered," Carlos said with a dismissive wave of his hand. "You just sit there and think up more 'sinister' stories. When I get back with our drinks, you can tell me all about them."

7.

Everything changed the summer Nick turned fourteen. The Missouri heat roiled against the windows like a living thing, blistering the house and stopping time. School had ended in a blur of signatures in yearbooks and promises to keep in touch that everyone knew were lies. His mother had been away again, at another conference with Susan—always with Susan now, always for "work" they claimed, though Nick had started to understand something else happening there, something the adults thought he'd been too young to see.

Gene stayed at home more than usual that summer. He'd lost another job at another garage—something about a customer's complaint, though he never said what happened. Gene's jobs were like that: vague explanations, quick departures, long stretches of unemployment, and promises that the next job would be different. With Gene there all day, the house took on a new life, like a creature holding its breath. Each room became a space to navigate, each doorway a potential trap, each corner holding its own specific kind of terror.

There was a ritual to Gene's predatory advancements. Always a ritual, like church but twisted into something dark and secret. Nick learned to read the signs, to sense him coming, the way animals can sense a storm approaching. The way the air would change, the way sounds would shift, the way time itself slowed and stretched like taffy. The progression had been calculated: At twelve, Nick could explain away Gene's first soft touches and the harder caresses that left bruises. By thirteen, Nick had learned to endure the rough massages in silence. For three years, he had carried the secrets, until Jason's accusations at fifteen finally sent him to Aunt Julia's. And by then, the damage had been done.

Gene's patience made him dangerous. That was the thing nobody understood about him. He could wait for hours, hold still until the conditions were just right—until the house settled into that specific afternoon quiet, until the neighborhood sounds faded to distant echoes. Lawn mowers buzzed two streets over, children laughed in backyard pools, cars passed with windows down, radios spilled summer songs—all sounds that merged into a background hum, making the silence inside the house feel even more absolute, deafening.

"Come here, Nicholas." The words would float up the stairs or through the screen door or across the kitchen. Gene's voice would be calm, casual, almost gentle. Not angry, since anger would have been easier to understand, easier to fight against. Not threatening—threats would have given Nick something to grab onto, something to prove he wasn't crazy for being afraid. His father's voice was just matter-of-fact, like commenting on the weather or asking about homework. As if what was about to happen was as normal as helping with yard work or taking out the trash or any of the other ordinary things fathers asked their sons to do.

And fighting only made the outcome worse. Resistance was blood in the water, weakness seeping through the cracks. Compliance became armor, a means to make it end faster. Nick developed strategies, small survival tricks. Sitting still, he focused on details—the pattern of the wallpaper, dust motes drifting in sunbeams, the ticking clock on the wall. He learned to disconnect, to float above his own body, like mist over frozen ground. He became less than himself—fading, empty, nothing at all. A boy-shaped absence in the room where a person used to be.

8.

"Well?" Carlos held fresh drinks.

Nick took the glass from his hand, hands that were soft and warm. Carlos's touch—gentle, asking, present—was nothing like Gene's. And that difference terrified Nick more than anything else.

Carlos had brought Nick a double on the rocks this time. Was it a silent acknowledgment of how much he had drunk the first round? Or a calculated move to get him into bed? Did Nick even care?

"I said, 'well?'"

"Well, what?"

"Have you thought of it? Some other 'sinister' thing?"

Nick took a sip of his new tequila. Then another. He didn't answer, and Carlos didn't press him. Nick was starting to appreciate Carlos's short attention span—something that might have irritated him on any other day. But tonight, he let Carlos believe his mind remained empty, a blank slate, like one of the stereotypical dumb blondes filling the bar.

In truth, something darker churned beneath Nick's practiced indifference. After Laslo, after those paintings documenting years of violation, he should have been anywhere but here. Yet here he stood, in the kind of bar where men disappeared with strangers, where touch came with a price tag, where the darkness made everyone complicit. He had made himself into the kind of target that attracted a certain type of attention.

Tonight should have been simple: Get drunk and find someone rough, someone who wanted to use him, someone who would confirm everything he believed about men and touch and his own worthlessness. He would find someone like Laslo, but this time, Nick would choose. This time, he'd walk into the violation with open eyes.

But Carlos refused to play his part. His gentle questions mixed with playfulness, his obvious tenderness, his careful attention to Nick's wants—these were more threatening than aggression ever could be. Nick had braced himself for violence. He wasn't prepared for the possibility of something else, the idea that connection could be real. Better to keep drinking, to push Carlos away, to find someone who would hurt him properly.

But something dark and grudge-holding was lifting from Nick. Without warning, a nervous urge rose in him—to shout that he held something back, that he knew and felt something that explained his timidity and awkwardness, words that rose in his throat like bile: "My father is dead!" Suddenly, he wanted to scream, to let the truth burst forth and shatter this careful facade. The single fact that could explain everything: every flinch, every hesitation, every intentional word. His mouth opened, the confession perched on his lips—

"Somebody told me about a film showing at the Cinémathèque Française. A gay-themed one, apparently. Something about two men who meet and spend a weekend together. Tom Cullen's the lead, if I remember correctly. Have you—"

Nick's jaw clenched, and his fingers dug into the glass, gripping until his knuckles went white. One more squeeze and he might shatter the glass altogether, sending shards across the bar. The pain might have even felt good. But Carlos had already moved on, talking about some film.

"*Weekend*. From 2011."

Nick only half-listened but was smart enough to keep up with two things at once, for appearance's sake anyway.

"Yes, *Weekend*. Tom Cullen and, what's-his-name, Chris New, I think. Who really is gay in real life. It's showing in Bercy on Tuesday, I—"

At once, Nick's mind leapt into technicolor. "Who's the person you were talking to earlier?"

"What?"

"I said, who were you talking to on the phone earlier?"

"Nosy much?"

Nick winced, sorry he'd asked and even sorrier for the tone Carlos had taken. Nick put his drink down and reached for his jacket, balled up in one corner of the bench. Nearby, a boy of no more than nineteen laughed hysterically. Rain continued to patter and mingle with the loud thump-thump of the heavy R&B. The shirtless bartender dropped a spoon on the metal work surface. All the noise threatened to do Nick's head in. He looked at his watch: 9 p.m. The worrying sense that he'd spend the rest of the night home alone momentarily kept him from putting his jacket on. He'd just picked it up again when Carlos's hand grazed his thigh again.

"You're not going, are you?"

Nick wrapped his scarf around his neck.

"It was my son, alright."

"Your son?"

"Yeah, he's twelve. Just a kid."

"Twelve," Nick repeated. "And your wife?"

"Ex."

"Ex?"

"He lives with her. My son. He lives with my ex-wife."

"But the way you spoke to him...," Nick began, trying to put the pieces together. "It was soft, gentle. I don't know, I assumed a *lover*, I guess..."

"Well, he is the love of my life, you could say."

The tears came unbidden, silent betrayers that Nick could only hide by bowing his head. Drops of condensation bled into his drink, and each mouthful of watered-down tequila carried him closer to an edge he recognized too well, a precipice both magnetic and terrifying. Laslo should have taught him better. Broken people could mistake shared wounds for intimacy, could transform the desperate need to be understood into something raw and hungry and wrong.

And he had been wrong about Carlos—the raging storm of Nick's mind had been calmed by a single sentence, and the weight of a dozen or more years lifted in a mere moment. That phone call of soft words, genuine love, and uncomplicated care revealed a world Nick had heard about but never known. A world where fathers loved their sons without condition or cost, where touch didn't have to mean taking.

The music throbbed around them with an insistent beat, and Nick felt that familiar dissociation creeping in—the sensation of floating he'd honed to perfection in Gene's workshop. But Carlos's hand, firm on his thigh, yanked him back to reality, each gentle touch a jolt that grounded him here, making a choice. If he stayed, if he allowed this man to be kind, he'd have to confront the harrowing possibility that not every touch was a weapon, that not every connection was a trap waiting to ensnare him. He was dodging a different truth now, one no longer centered on Gene, nor even on his mother. The shift was inward, focusing on himself—on the reasons he had entered this bar, driven by a need for punishment. He sought out a confrontation that would validate his father's harsh teachings about love, pain, and his own worth. Yet, as he sat there, torn, he questioned if he believed he deserved such a fate.

Nick leaned against the wall, his eyes following the ebb and flow of the crowd on the dance floor. The bodies, swaying together and apart in a seamless wave of motion, moved to the pounding beat. The air wafted with the scent of sweat and cologne, and the flashing lights painted everything in shades of blue and red. Those boys in their tank tops, laughing, dancing, reaching for each other without fear—they belonged to a different species, a stark contrast to the caution that had become his second nature. In Gene's workshop, he had learned how touch could be manipulated and twisted, and those lessons lingered like ghosts in his mind.

Beside him, Carlos continued his monologue, his voice steady and relaxed, and talked about his son with a tenderness that pierced Nick with a thousand tiny acupuncture needles. Carlos spoke of shared custody battles, the joy of weekend visits, and the simple happiness of flipping pancakes together on Sunday mornings, the sweet scent of batter and syrup. Each word dug deeper into Nick's consciousness, a reminder of the life he had never known. He'd imagined meeting someone like Laslo in this bar—instead, he found himself confronted by Carlos, a father who cherished his child with a love so genuine and untainted.

A bolt of thunder crashed through the beat of the music, and Nick felt a primal urge to flee. But something else came with that flash: a dangerous spark of wanting. Not just for Carlos's body, but for what he represented: the possibility that not every touch had to leave a mark, that not every connection had to be transactional.

"Seems like something is wrong." Carlos leaned closer. "Are you alright?"

Nick shook his head, unable to find the words. How could he explain the turmoil inside him? The conflicting desires to both flee and to lean in?

"I shouldn't be here," Nick mumbled.

"Why not?" Carlos asked. His hand remained on Nick's thigh.

Nick took a shaky breath. "I came here looking for… something else. Something not good for me. And you're…" He trailed off.

"I'm what?" Carlos coaxed.

"You're nice. I don't know how to handle that."

Carlos studied Nick's face, worry creeping into his eyes. He moved closer through the thrum of music until their conversation became a soft melody of its own.

"What were you looking for, Nick? What did you come here hoping to find?"

Nick's throat tightened, constricting like a vise. Though the storm inside him defied language, its meaning was clear. He had not tumbled into this smoke-filled bar for solace. He'd come seeking punishment, a cruel affirmation of his own perceived worthlessness. After everything with his father and Laslo, he believed pain was the only currency he was worth trading in.

"I don't know," he lied. Unable to meet Carlos's searching gaze, Nick fixated on the worn wood of the bar counter. "Just… not this. Not someone like you."

Carlos paused, his thumb tracing small, soothing circles on Nick's thigh—a quiet gesture of comfort that sent faint ripples across Nick's skin. "I think you do know. And I think you're scared of the answer."

Nick's head snapped up, his eyes locking onto Carlos's. No judgment lingered there—only a calm, deep understanding that reached into Nick's soul, making his chest ache with an unfamiliar yearning for acceptance. When Carlos spoke, his voice carried both gentleness and unwavering firmness, resonating with a tender cadence.

"I'm not..." Nick started, but the lie died on his lips. He took a shaky breath. "You're right. I am scared."

Carlos nodded, his hand still moving on Nick's leg. "Do you want to talk about it?"

Nick barked out a harsh laugh. "God, no. That's the last thing I want."

"Okay. We don't have to talk. We can just sit here, if you'd like. Or cuddle. Or leave. Whatever you want."

Nick winced, unsettled. He had braced for Carlos to push or pry. This simple acceptance felt strange, even wrong, as if kindness without conditions was something Nick had forgotten how to recognize.

9.

Marc scrubbed at a wine stain on his kitchen worktop, though the stain had been there for years. The usual precision of his movements had given way to freneticism, a near violence in his wild motions. The cleaning supplies he'd bought at the supermarket earlier—three different kinds of bleach, specialty stone cleaner, new sponges—were lined up with military precision along the edge of the sink.

The apartment smelled of chemicals and shame. He'd been cleaning for hours, since Susan had left his messages unanswered, since Lynne had called him crying about the scene in Nick's apartment. The bathroom gleamed. The windows sparkled. For the first time in a very long time, his apartment felt almost like something to be proud of. But the wine stain wouldn't lift, dark against the cheap laminate like a lingering regret.

His hands had gone red and chapped from cleaning, his expensive manicure ruined. Somewhere behind him, his phone pinged again—messages he hoped were updates from Susan about Lynne, about Nick, about the funeral arrangements, about anything to disrupt this cleansing routine. But he couldn't stop scrubbing. Couldn't stop trying to erase something that had soaked too deep to ever come out.

He remembered another stain, years ago in Missouri, a pool of red wine on Lynne's cream carpet. The night Lynne had decided to send Nick to his aunt's. How they'd all pretended not to see what was happening—no one ever believed Nick had done those things to Jason. But they'd focused on blotting the carpet instead of questioning why a teenager needed to be sent away. Nick would be safer with Julia, Marc had thought at the time, safe from Gene. It was all such a mess: They had saved Nick from his abuser, but sent him away for being an abuser. *C'est quoi ce monde de merde?!*

Marc moved his step stool to the windows again, though he'd already cleaned them twice, his movements repetitive and confined. The glass squeaked under his cloth as he worked in tight circular motions. From this height, he could just about see the steeple of Saint-Sulpice, its towers stark against the afternoon sky—a view of freedom bordered by the very bars he now polished to gleaming. How many times had he sat there for Mass, trying to pray away his guilt, his knowledge, his own cowardice?

The apartment looked almost respectable now, like the kind of place someone like him should live. Someone who'd been born for the good life, who spoke a perfect, charming, sophisticated French, and who pretended to dine at the right restaurants and know all the right people. But underneath the harsh chemicals and polish remained a shabby little space above a noisy street, a prison full of stains that wouldn't come out.

His phone made another sound. He caught his reflection in the squeaky-clean window—hair unruly from the cleaning fumes, clothes spotted with bleach. What had he said to Nick at dinner? Something awful about being radiant when angry. The same kind of thing Gene used to say to the boys. The same kind of crafted compliments that weren't compliments at all, but something darker.

The sound of children playing floated up from the street—the school across the way must have dismissed. Marc attacked the windows again, harder now, as if he could erase the memories along with the smudges.

He needed music, something to drown out the children's voices, the memories, his own thoughts. But his usual playlist of camp Europop felt wrong today. Everything felt wrong. He settled for the ambient noise of traffic and street life drifting up through the windows he'd just cleaned.

The bleach had soaked through his rubber gloves, his fingers tingling. He should stop, should eat something, should return Susan's calls—should do anything except continue this manic cleaning that wasn't about cleaning at all. But if he stopped, he'd have to think about Nick's face when he'd made those comments, about all the secrets everyone seemed good at keeping (until they weren't), and about how he'd become the kind of man he'd always despised. Being flirtatious was one thing, that was part of Marc's charm, but pushing things too far, to be so damn pretentious as to be cruel, was another.

The wine stain on the worktop caught his eye again. He turned back to the dark spot, armed with a new cleaning product. This one promised to remove even the most stubborn stains, to make everything new again. But some things couldn't be made new. Some stains had deeper roots—like the stain of watching and doing nothing, of pretending not to see.

At last, his arm aching, Marc dropped the sponge into the sink. He stared at the wine stain—still there, still looming, still accusing. All that scrubbing had only managed to wear away the surrounding laminate, making the stain even more prominent against the damaged surface.

He opened a cabinet, moved aside the cleaning supplies he'd arranged in neat rows, and pulled out a bottle of Bordeaux. Not his usual expensive taste, but the cheap stuff he kept hidden in the back, the kind he drank alone when he didn't have to perform sophistication for anyone else.

The cork came out with a soft pop that echoed in the spotless kitchen. He didn't bother with a glass but instead tilted the bottle to his lips. A few drops fell on the stain, the new wine mixing with the old mark, spreading outward like a blooming flower. Like spilled secrets. Like guilt.

"*À ta santé*," he muttered—to Gene, to Jason, to Nick, to his own reflection in the spotless windows. He drank deeply, letting the wine drip down onto his bleach-spotted shirt, onto the worktop, onto everything he'd spent all day trying and failing to make pure.

He caught his own eye in the window's reflection. Even now, he couldn't help noticing how he held the bottle: wrist cocked just so, as if this weren't Monop' bottom-shelf shit but rather something worth savoring. Always performing, even alone. That's what Lynne had said to him once upon a time: "For God's sake, Marc, who are you trying to impress in your own kitchen?" He'd found that ironic at the time, coming from her. But like recognizes like, and more truth lived in Lynne's words than even she realized.

Trying to impress everyone, always. Lynne had been right. The careful way he pronounced the names of vineyards at restaurants (and always pretended he had visited them), the little lectures about proper stemware that nobody had asked for, the way he'd hover over guests' shoulders suggesting the perfect pairings—as if any of it made him more than what he was: a lonely middle-aged man.

He took a swig, deliberately messy this time. Nick had seen right through him. That slight arch of the eyebrow when Marc had corrected his pronunciation of "Moët," that flickering smile that said *I know what you are.* A fraud. A counterfeit. A man so desperate to be sophisticated that he'd become a caricature of sophistication.

He took another long drink, the wine bitter on his tongue. Gene had been a mean drunk—not that Marc had any right to judge, not tonight. But God, he could still see Nick at eleven, with a split lip, Lynne passing it off as a playground accident. And there Marc had been, all these years later, playing sophisticated wine snob, as if any of that mattered, as if that's what Nick or Lynne needed from him.

The wine burned down his throat. He set the bottle down carefully—even now, he noticed his carefulness—and looked at his hands. Still tingling from the bleach, pink and raw with a persistent shake. He'd spent so many years trying to be someone else, someone better, someone who knew wine vintages and collected bottles, not someone who worried about meeting his monthly rent. He was not only a counterfeit—he was cruel.

He picked up the bottle again and poured the rest down the sink, watching the ruby liquid spiral away. Then he reached for the glass cleaner. The windows weren't yet clean enough.

10.

Carlos traced patterns on Nick's bare shoulder. Nick shivered at Carlos's touch, so unlike anything he'd known before. Gentle. Asking, not taking. In the dim light of Carlos's bedroom, Nick could almost believe this normalcy was his. That touch could mean comfort instead of violation. He closed his eyes, fighting the urge to pull away, to protect himself from this unfamiliar tenderness.

The rain had followed them home, kissing the windows with a steady hush. Thunder rolled in the distance, a low growl echoing the upheaval in Nick's chest. Carlos flicked on a lamp. Its warm light revealed a soft leather chair that had clearly been his favorite spot for years. Carlos's apartment, Nick noticed, was a refuge of quiet functionality: A low side table bore marks on its legs—the kind made by a child's roughhousing. Blackout curtains spoke of someone who valued sleep. On the wall, a crayon drawing of a dinosaur hung in a real frame next to what looked like an actual Basquiat print, given equal prominence. This was a space shaped by real life, by the rhythms of part-time parenthood.

"You're trembling." Carlos's fingers paused on Nick's skin. The amber glow of a streetlamp filtered through the streaked windows. "We don't have to—"

"No," Nick said double-quick, then softer. "No. It's just..." He thought of the letter sitting in his jacket pocket, of his father's face—twisted with disgust—the last time he'd seen him. Of all the years between then and now, Nick had learned to make himself small, untouchable. "I'm not used to this."

Carlos shifted closer. The mattress dipped beneath his weight. Warm and steady as a heartbeat, his palm came to rest flat against Nick's back. "To what?"

The kindness in his voice made Nick's throat tight. "To being touched like I matter."

Carlos pecked a soft kiss to Nick's temple. "You're thinking too hard."

This tenderness terrified Nick more than any aggression. He didn't know how to be touched like this—like he mattered, like he was worthy of care.

"I shouldn't be here," Nick said, echoing his words from the bar.

"You keep saying that. Do you want to leave?"

The silence stretched, heavy with his unspoken answer. Nick knew he should say yes, should grab his clothes and flee into the rainy night. Return to his empty apartment and the crushing weight of everything he desperately wanted to outrun. But the gentle rise and fall of Carlos's chest kept Nick anchored to the moment.

The words caught in Nick's throat before breaking free. "No, I don't want to leave."

Carlos nodded, resuming his soft caresses. "Then stay."

Nick played with his fingers, twisting and untwisting them, putting them to his mouth, biting his nails, a nervous energy that morphed into nervous tension between him and Carlos. Nick wondered if Carlos could read his mind, see his thoughts. Could anyone be that perceptive?

For a moment, Nick surrendered to a familiar ritual of self-sabotage, conjuring the image of another man from earlier that evening: a specter in navy blue who had haunted the far corner of the bar like a warning light. The stranger's shirt had hung open, an indigo wound against the smoke-dimmed air, and Nick recalled how the man had put on a show of removing the shirt to display a perfect physique. Nick had watched him from across the room with the detached fascination of someone studying their own reflection in a funhouse mirror, saw in him all the possibilities of what this night could become, or fail to become.

But his attention returned to the present, to Carlos, who sat watching him with that serene smile. *This is someone I could change my life for*, Nick thought, then caught himself, questioning this sudden impulse. What he wanted, he reminded himself, was someone who could make him forget everything else: his worries, his past, all of it. Wasn't it?

Yet even as Carlos sat there, as present as gravity, Nick's mind began crafting elegies for their unborn future. He saw himself wandering through phantom February twilights, when the city turned to wet slate and loneliness echoed in empty stairwells. His imagination, that treacherous architect, could build entire worlds from fragments that didn't yet exist: morning light streaming through Carlos's window, catching solar confetti above a bed he'd never slept in; the brass song of a coffee grinder he'd never heard; the metallic symphony of door locks and security chains that would mark their eventual separate lives. Nick was already becoming nostalgic for memories he hadn't made, mourning the loss of moments that existed only in the dark gallery of his fears.

He recognized this habit of his, this compulsion to preserve himself by racing to the end, like a reader who flips to a book's final page to protect himself from becoming too invested in the story. He was a shipwrecked soul, who, spotting salvation on the horizon, refused to believe in rescue. Someone who had learned to find comfort in the predictable dangers of his isolation—the snakes, the solitude, the endless empty beaches—rather than risk the unknown perils of hope. *Maybe being alone isn't so bad after all*, he thought. Perhaps if he convinced himself he'd already lost Carlos, he could act natural. But Nick's apprehension tangled with his performance, vulnerable in both truth and theater. Another greater part of him wanted to look away, feigning distraction. He wanted Carlos to notice and worry about losing him, just as Nick feared losing Carlos. Or maybe, he wanted Carlos to see through this act and laugh at it, to recognize these familiar games of pretend indifference, these games that perhaps Carlos himself played.

They lay in silence for a while, raindrops providing a soothing backdrop. Nick allowed himself to relax little by little, his body unclenching from its defensive posture. He couldn't remember the last time he'd been touched like this—without agenda, without pain. Maybe never.

"Can I ask you something?"

Nick tensed again, bracing himself. "Okay."

"You don't have to answer if you don't want to," Carlos said. "But earlier, at the bar, what were you thinking about?"

Nick's breath caught in his throat. Images flashed through his mind—his father's workshop, Laslo's paintings, all the dark places he'd been trying to escape. He squeezed his eyes shut, willing the memories away. "It's complicated."

Carlos's hand stilled on Nick's shoulder. "I'm listening, if you want to talk."

Nick turned away, wrestling with himself. Part of him wanted to flee, to keep his secrets locked away. But another part, a part he could just about recognize, longed to unburden himself. To let someone else carry even a fraction of the weight he'd been bearing alone for years.

"My father died," Nick said, the words scraping against his throat.

Carlos's expression shifted. "I'm sorry," he said. "That's… that's really awful."

Nick nodded. "Yeah. But it's… complicated."

"Complicated how?" Carlos asked, concerned.

Nick stared at his hands. "My father wasn't a good man. He… hurt me. For years. I thought his death would free me, but I just feel… lost."

Carlos pulled Nick closer, enveloping him in a gentle embrace. "I'm so sorry that happened to you," Carlos said. "No child should ever have to go through that."

Nick's body tensed as if bracing for a blow that never came. The warmth of quiet acceptance wrapped around him—no demands, no judgment, just presence. His breath hitched, chest tightening as memories stirred at the edges of his mind, threatening to pull him under.

"I don't even know why I'm telling you all of this," Nick mumbled, avoiding eye contact. But as his words spilled out, a sense of relief washed over him. He hadn't expected this, hadn't come looking for understanding or comfort.

Nick shifted, his body tensing. "I really should go."

But Carlos didn't let go. "You don't have to leave. Not unless you want to."

The tenderness cracked something in Nick's chest. He squeezed his eyes shut, willing himself not to cry.

"I don't know how to do this," Nick admitted. "How to be touched without… without it hurting."

Carlos's hand stroked Nick's hair. "We don't have to do anything you're not comfortable with. We can just lie here if you want."

"I was twelve when it started," Nick said, the words feeling strange on his tongue. "Three years of…" He stopped, unable to finish. "Sometimes I think about those years between twelve and fifteen, and they feel like a lifetime."

Carlos didn't speak, just kept his hand steady on Nick's back, his breath even and calm. The silence held no expectation, no demand for words or explanations. Carlos's quiet presence was nothing like the heavy silences of Nick's childhood—the ones that pressed down like stones, crushing him until he broke.

Being held, being touched without pain or expectation, was alien and raw. Part of Nick wanted to flee, to retreat to the familiar darkness. But another part, a part he didn't recognize, ached to stay in this moment of tender grace.

The rain tapped against the windows as Nick's muscles released, his body uncoiling from its defensive curl. Carlos's heartbeat and warm breath anchored him to the present.

"Thank you," Nick said, his voice quiet. "For not pushing. For just… being here."

Carlos took Nick's hand into his own. "Let's just lie here."

Nick nestled closer to Carlos, allowing himself to be enveloped in the comfort of another person's touch. For the first time in years—maybe ever—he felt safe. A fragile peace settled over him as his racing thoughts began to quiet, the ever-present tension melting from his bones. He focused on the steady rise and fall of Carlos's chest, the rhythm a gentle anchor, even as emotion welled up in his throat. This unexpected compassion made him want to weep for all he'd never known, and yet the steady beat of Carlos's heart promised something he'd never dared to hope for: sanctuary.

11.

The crash shattered the silence—a deafening explosion of glass and liquid that sent shards skittering across the carpet like shrapnel. Lynne froze, wondering if she could somehow rewind the seconds. Wine pooled around her feet, dark and viscous, and seeped into the thin hotel carpet. Hitting her like a slap, the acrid, sharp scent mingled with the lingering traces of her own unwashed despair. She stared at the broken bottle, her chest heaving, her mind spiraling. The wine spread like blood—Gene's blood, she thought hysterically—an ever-widening stain she couldn't contain, couldn't control, couldn't hide anymore.

"It's just a bottle," she said to herself, her voice hoarse, unconvincing. "Just a bottle." But even those words tasted like lies in her mouth, each syllable bitter as the spilled wine. Everything was falling apart, a deterioration that had begun many years ago, and now she couldn't even hold onto a simple bottle without destroying it.

The sirens outside—louder now, closer—told her otherwise. They weren't just sirens; they were a verdict. In her mind's eye, she pictured the scene: the officers storming in, their faces stern, their hands cuffed. They know. They know what you've done. What kind of mother you are. What kind of mother lets her husband hurt their sons? What kind of mother sends one away and loses the other to suicide? The questions battered against her skull like angry wasps.

Her voice cracked: "No, no, no." Her hands flew to her head, fingers tangling in her greasy hair, which she pulled until pain sparked across her scalp. The weight of it—the shame, the guilt, twenty years of carefully maintained silence—pummeled her chest. She couldn't breathe. The room's walls seemed to pulse inward, closing around her like a fist. "They're coming for me. They're coming to take me away." And maybe they should. Maybe that's what she deserved.

Susan appeared in an instant, her presence cutting through the haze like a blade. She didn't speak—didn't need to. Her hands were firm, unyielding, as she grabbed Lynne by the shoulders and steered her toward the bathroom. Lynne stumbled, her legs unsteady, her breath coming in ragged gasps. The carpet beneath her feet shifted like quicksand, each step threatening to pull her under.

"Susan, they're here," Lynne choked out. The words tasted like ash in her mouth. Her throat closed around the things she'd never said, confessions that fought to escape all at once. "They're going to arrest me. I can't—I can't—" Can't face it. Can't hide anymore. Can't keep pretending.

"Shut up," Susan snapped, her tone sharp but not unkind. She shoved Lynne into the bathroom, the door slamming shut behind them with the finality of a prison cell. The fluorescent light buzzed overhead like angry insects and cast a harsh, unforgiving glow on Lynne's pale, gaunt face in the mirror. She caught a glimpse of herself and recoiled—a stranger stared back, sunken-eyed and haunted. Is this what Nick saw when he looked at her? This ghost of a mother, this shell of a woman?

The bathroom pressed in around them, too small for their shared history, for all the things left unsaid. With nowhere to go, the steam from the shower collected on the mirror, the walls, their skin. Susan's reflection fractured and multiplied in the fogged glass, a chorus of silent judges. The cold tile floor seeped through Lynne's stockings. Everything felt simultaneously too sharp and too distant, like a dream she couldn't wake from.

Susan's nose wrinkled as the stench hit her—sour, unwashed skin, the tang of sweat and alcohol, the bitter perfume of grief. She looked at Lynne, really looked at her, and what she saw made her stomach twist: Lynne's hollow eyes, her greying cheeks cut out like a skull, makeup smeared in dark bruise-like circles. She looked… monstrous. Broken. Like something that had crawled out of the dark space between mother and murderer.

"You're not going anywhere," Susan said, her voice low, commanding. The words bounced off the tiled walls, echoing in the small space until they seemed to come from everywhere at once. "Not like this."

Lynne's breath stalled, her chest heaving as she stared at Susan like a cornered animal. The mirror behind them reflected infinite versions of this moment—the strong one and the broken one, multiplied forever in fractured glass. "You don't understand," she said, her voice cracking. Her fingers clawed at her own arms, jagged red paths trailing her pale skin. "I'm a terrible mother. I'm—I'm—" The words wouldn't come. How could they? How could any words contain the magnitude of her failure?

"Stop," Susan interrupted, her voice cutting through Lynne's spiraling thoughts. She stepped closer, her hands gripping Lynne's shoulders again, grounding her. The small bathroom blurred their reflections together in the mirror, past and present colliding in the steam. "You're not. You're just… lost." The words, heavy as the damp air, hung between them.

Lynne's eyes filled with tears, but she didn't fight back. She just stood there, shaking, as Susan took control. And for the first time in what felt like forever, she let someone else hold the reins. Her body sagged, strings cut, all those years of holding herself together finally snapping under the weight of Gene's death, of Nick's anger, of Jason's absence.

The bathroom cramped around them like a confessional box, sweat and stale wine thickening the air until breathing became drowning. Susan peeled Lynne's damp shirt away with mechanical precision. The fabric clung like a second skin, and Lynne flinched as Susan pulled her free. Lynne's clammy, pale flesh glowed under the harsh fluorescent light, and she looked like something half-formed, a creature caught between states. Susan kept silent. Words felt useless now, like water slipping through cupped hands.

The mirror had completely fogged over, turning their reflections into smeared ghosts. The clouded glass revealed her in crimson-edged pieces, fragments of a woman she barely recognized. When had she become this insipid thing, this failed mother, this keeper of terrible secrets? The steam's accusatory hands pressed against her skin.

She turned the shower handle. The pipes groaned deep in the walls, a sound like distant screaming. Cold water rushed from the nozzle in a silver sheet. Lynne's eyes widened as Susan guided her toward the spray. "Step in," Susan said, steady but soft, the voice of one coaxing a frightened animal. Lynne hesitated, her body stiff with resistance, but Susan maintained her firm grip. The wet tile slicked beneath Lynne's feet, treacherous as memory.

The first icy droplets hit her skin, and she gasped, her shoulders jerking as if she'd been struck. The cold shot through her like lightning, shocking her nerve endings alive. Susan didn't let go. She stood there, her own clothes soaking through, watching as Lynne shivered under the relentless stream. For a second, Lynne's hands clawed at the air as she searched for something to hold onto, but then they fell limp at her sides. Her breath came in shallow bursts, her chest rising and falling like a wounded creature. The water, running in rivulets down her face, was indistinguishable from tears.

The shower's spray bounced off the tiles and filled the small space with a fine mist. Lynne remembered fog rolling off the Missouri River in a similar way, the kind of fog that swallowed their house whole on autumn mornings. She'd liked those days, when the world beyond their windows disappeared and she could pretend nothing existed outside their four walls. But the fog had hidden things too: the neighbors' concerned glances, red and purple bruises on her boys' skin, the truth she didn't want to see.

Still, Susan stayed silent, her presence the single cool point in the inferno of Lynne's thoughts. Words would come later, if they came at all. For now, the cold water, the steam, the echoing bathroom with its accusatory mirror and flickering light dominated. A purgatory of her own making.

When she was sure Lynne wouldn't collapse, Susan stepped back. The mess of the hotel room—shards of glass glinting like broken teeth on the carpet, the burgundy stain spreading like a wound—were evidence of all the things she couldn't fix. Susan ignored the disarray. Her fingers fumbled as she filled the kettle at the sink, muscle memory taking over where conscious thought failed. The mundane act of making tea felt absurd, almost laughable, given the wreckage around her. But she needed it, needed something to anchor her before she drowned in the chaos too. The familiar ritual—fill, click, wait—gave her something to focus on besides the sound of Lynne's ragged breathing from behind the bathroom door.

The kettle clicked on, and her mind ignited, thoughts sparking and catching like wildfire racing through dry bush. How did we get here? The question burned through her, sharp and unrelenting. She thought of Lynne—her Lynne—a woman who had once blazed through life and laughed like sunlight breaking through clouds. The woman who'd challenged department heads and fought for tenure and dared to love another woman in a world that hadn't been ready for such love. Now, that woman smoldered in the ruins of their life, hollowed out by guilt and grief, her edges splintered and raw.

And Susan? She held the pieces together with nothing but sheer will, her own hands bleeding from the effort. Every time she thought they'd escaped the past together, something would trigger Lynne—a news story about abuse, a photo of Jason, a chance encounter with someone from Missouri—and they'd be right back here. Susan cleaning up the mess while Lynne spun apart, both of them pretending they could outrun their shadows.

The kettle's whistle built slowly, a thin sound that grew to a scream. Steam erupted from its spout like an accusation. With shaking hands, Susan poured hot water over the tea bag and watched the water turn golden-brown. The scent rose between her cupped palms, familiar and foreign at once. How many cups of tea had she made like this? How many times had she tried to fix things with carefully steeped hibiscus and honey?

Steam and silence fogged the bathroom when Susan stepped back in, clutching the mug of tea like a talisman. Its fragrance pierced the damp air—rooibos, sugar, a futile attempt at comfort. The shower's spray had reduced to a thin trickle, each drop echoing against the tile like a metronome counting down.

Lynne huddled on the shower floor, knees drawn to her chest, water coursing down her back. Her skin still glowed eerily under the harsh light, wet strands of hair plastering her face. She looked so, so small, something shattered and abandoned. The fluorescent bulb flickered once, twice, staining her hunched form in sickly bands of maroon and black.

Susan turned off the shower and crouched beside Lynne. Water soaked through Susan's slacks, but she barely noticed. She pushed the mug toward Susan as steam curled upward, ghost-like in the bathroom's artificial light. "Drink this. It'll help." Hollow words, inadequate comfort. As if tea could wash away decades of silence, of complicity, of carefully maintained lies.

Lynne didn't move at first, her gaze fixed on some distant point beyond the tiles. Her hands rested limply on her knees, fingers twitching as if trying to grasp something not there. The mirror behind them had started clearing in patches, revealing fragments of their reflection—Susan's rigid posture, Lynne's collapsed form, the stark light turning everything harsh and unforgiving.

"Come on," Susan urged, her voice firmer now. She nudged the mug closer, the tea's surface trembling with the movement. "Just a sip. For me."

Lynne's eyes launched toward her, glassy and unfocused at first, then sharpening with a flicker of recognition—a spark in the void. Her eyes were rimmed in red, all that unshed grief finally finding its color. She reached out, her fingers brushing the mug. Susan guided the cup to her lips, and Lynne took a tentative sip, then another. The warmth seemed to seep into her, her shoulders relaxing ever so little. But her hands still shook, ripples spreading across the tea's surface like aftershocks.

"That's it," Susan said. "You're here. You're with me." The words bounced off the tiled walls, coming back to them distorted. Here, but for how long? With me, but how completely?

Later, when Susan had wrapped Lynne in one of the hotel's thin robes and guided her to the bed, the room grew too quiet. The weight of all their mistakes hung like an oppressive smog, thick and choking around them. The wine stain on the carpet had dried to a dark flower, its edges crisp and condemning. With her arms crossed over her chest, Susan stood by the window and stared out at the city below. Lights flashed through the streaked glass, Paris transformed into a watercolor of neon and shadow.

The space between them felt vast and treacherous, filled with all the things they'd never said. The soft whir of the hotel's air conditioning couldn't mask the tension that crackled like exposed wires. Lynne, perched on the edge of the bed, clean and wrapped in the robe, appeared somehow more vulnerable than she'd been in the shower. Her hair had begun to dry in uneven waves, the look of someone younger, more fragile. Her fingers worried the hem of her sleeve, pulling at a loose thread until the stitching started to unravel.

"We can't go," Susan said at last, her voice low but steady. She didn't turn from the window, couldn't bear to see Lynne's face as she continued. "Not to Gene's funeral. And not to Cape Town."

Lynne's head snapped up, her eyes wide with something between panic and relief. "What? Why not?" The words came out scratchy, her throat still raw from crying.

Susan turned then, forcing herself to meet Lynne's gaze. The city lights cast strange shadows across her face as she moved. "Because you're not ready. And neither am I. We're drowning, Lynne. We can't keep pretending we're not."

The truth hung between them like smoke. They'd been running for so long—from Missouri, from memories, from consequences. Each new city, each fresh start, had been another layer of denial wrapped around them like a cocoon. But cocoons were meant to be broken, weren't they? Sometimes transformation required destruction first.

Lynne's hands tightened into fists, the bedsheet crumpling under her grip. Her knuckles turned white, and Susan could see the sharp sting of her nails biting into her palms. "Nick." Just his name sent a visible jolt through her chest, a live wire sparking in the dark. She shook her head, her voice hoarse. "No. I can't. You don't understand. I can't fix it with him. Not after… not after everything."

The words came out in a rush, ragged and uneven, as if they'd been torn from her throat. The air in the room grew heavier and heavier, suffocating. Memories flashed across Lynne's face—Nick's expression when she'd told him about Gene, the way he'd looked at her like she was a stranger, someone he didn't even recognize anymore.

Susan stepped closer, her presence falling over Lynne like a shadow. Her face stone, her jaw clenched, but her eyes—those deep, familiar eyes—soft and pleading. "You have to. This doesn't end until you fix it with him. There's no other way, Lynne. You know that."

Lynne's stomach twisted, a knot of nausea rising in her throat. She wanted to scream, to lash out, to bury herself under the covers and never come out. But Susan's gaze held her there, pinned like a butterfly on a board. The questions spilled out, harsh and desperate: "Why? Why does it have to be him? Why can't we just… move on?"

"Because you haven't," Susan shot back, her tone sharper now. "You're still stuck there, Lynne. In the past. With him. And until you face him, until you make it right, we're never going to move forward." She paused, her voice softening. "Do you think I want this? Do you think I want to watch you tear yourself apart over something that happened years ago?"

Lynne's chest ached with a dull, throbbing pain that spread

through her ribs, through her lungs, through her heart. She looked down at her trembling hands—hands that had once cradled her sons, that had packed Nick's bags for Connecticut, that had signed Jason's death certificate. When had they become so weak? When had she become so weak?

Susan knelt in front of her, reaching for those shaking hands. But Lynne wanted to pull away, to retreat into the numbness that had kept her safe for so long.

"Call him," Susan said, her voice firm but gentle. She pressed Lynne's phone into her palm. "Right now. Call him and fix this. For us. For you."

Lynne closed her eyes as tears spilled down her cheeks. She wanted to say no, to refuse, to curl up and disappear into the hotel's cheap sheets and never emerge. But Susan's hands were still holding hers, anchoring her to the moment, to the woman who had stayed when everyone else hadn't. The phone felt impossibly heavy between them, weighty with secrets and shame.

"Okay." She surrendered. "Okay."

Susan's voice left little room for negotiation: "Do it now. Before you talk yourself out of it."

The phone's glow etched her face in cold light, highlighted every wrinkle, every year, every regret. She hesitated before the final digit, her thumb hovering over the keypad. This is it, she thought, the words echoing in her mind like a death knell. No turning back. She swallowed hard, her throat dry as desert sand. Her thumb stilled, suspended. What if he doesn't answer? The thought sent ice through her veins. What if he does? That was somehow worse. The questions tangled in her mind, each one searing more than the last. She glanced at Susan, searching for something—reassurance, permission to stop, a way out—but Susan remained immovable, her lips pressed into a thin line.

The ringing began, sharp and metallic in Lynne's ear. Each tone sliced through the silence like a blade. Her heart hammered against her ribs so hard she felt sure Susan could see it trembling beneath her skin. She closed her eyes, trying to steady herself, but Nick's face—his anger, his disappointment, the way he'd looked at her when she'd finally told him about Gene's death—popped up again and again. Panic rose in her throat. But then, like a flicker of light in the dark, another thought surfaced—a sliver of hope, fragile and tentative as a spider's web. Maybe, just maybe, they could find their way back to each other.

The phone kept ringing. Lynne's grip tightened, her knuckles turning white. She teetered on the edge of something vast and uncharted, the ground beneath her shifting with every sharp, rhythmic chime. The sound filled her head, a pulsing loop of high-pitched beeps, cold and impersonal, demanding to be answered.

"It's going to be okay. You've got this," Susan said, her presence solid and grounding.

Lynne nodded, though she couldn't be sure she believed it. The ringing stopped. A beat of silence stretched thin between one heartbeat and the next. Then, a voice—deep, familiar, and distant. So distant.

"Hello?"

Lynne froze. Her mouth opened, but no words came out. She glanced at Susan, who gave her a small, encouraging nod. Lynne exhaled a shaky breath from somewhere deep beneath all her carefully constructed defenses.

"Nick, it's me."

A pause on the other end, heavy and loaded. But somewhere, deep down, hope flickered once more like a match struck in darkness, fragile but alive.

12.

Nick peered at his mother's name flashing on his phone screen. His thumb paused over the "decline" button. But something held him back—maybe the sting of the last few days or the fading warmth of Carlos's touch. He let the call ring once, twice, three times. Each chime tolled like grief given sound. On the fourth ring, something inside him broke. With a ragged breath, he swiped to answer.

"Hello?"

A pause, full of static, then: "Nick, it's me… it's Mom."

Closing his eyes, Nick leaned his forehead against the cool glass of the window. Outside, Paris continued its relentless dance of light, oblivious to the tempest raging within him.

"I'm so sorry, Nick. I should have told you sooner."

His free hand curled into a fist, fingers gathering hard into his palm, the bite of a tightening vice. "Yeah. You should have."

He could hear his mother's uneven breathing, could imagine her hunched over the phone, Susan hovering nearby.

"I want to—need to—explain." She rushed at the words, desperate. "About everything. Gene, Jason, about why you moved to Julia's… I know it's too late, but—"

"Which part?" Nick's voice cracked like a whip, unintended but unmistakable. "Which lie do you want to explain first?"

"That's not fair—"

"Fair?" A bitter laugh escaped him. "You want to talk about fair? You kept it from me. All day. Through dinner, through—"

"Nick, please."

"Do you know what it's like? To sit there eating fish while your father is dead? To find out—from Laslo—that Jason had come to Paris? That he was looking for me and that nobody told me?"

"We thought—"

"You thought. You always thought. You thought sending me to Aunt Julia's was best. You thought keeping Jason's letter from me—"

"I know. I was trying to protect—"

"No, don't say protect. Not that word."

Silence stretched between them, interrupted only by the flimsy sound of Lynne struggling to hold back tears.

"You're right," she said. "No, I wasn't trying to protect you. I was trying to protect myself."

Nick stayed silent, the phone still at his ear, shame and exhaustion knotted tight in his chest. Her words hung there, heavy and uneven, tugging at something he couldn't yet name. The tremor in her voice—different from the practiced steadiness he was so used to—made his throat constrict.

"I couldn't face it," she went on. "If I admitted what he was doing to you, I'd have to admit what he'd done to me. What I'd let him do to both of you by staying silent."

The phone shook in Nick's hand. "And you knew the whole time."

Why say this out loud, Nick suddenly thought. Why hash the details again and again? Yes, she knew, they all knew. But did the logistics really matter now?

"I knew and I didn't know," Lynne continued. "I suspected and I denied. I—" She was crying now, no longer hiding. "When Jason made those accusations against you, I grabbed onto Gene's solution like a lifeline. Sending you away. I told myself I was being strong, making the hard choice."

"Gene's solution?" Nick's voice dropped to sub-zero.

"He orchestrated all of it," Lynne said, finally letting herself understand. "Dropped little suggestions until I thought it was my idea. 'Some distance might help.' 'A fresh start.' And I was so desperate for someone to tell me what to do…" The tears cut through her words now. "And then Jason after he went to that college. Two months later…" She couldn't finish.

They sat in shared silence, connected by the phone line and the start of something else. Nick could hear her breathing, could picture her in that hotel room, could feel the weight of all those years pressing down on both of them.

"I don't know how to forgive you," Nick said.

"I'm not asking you to. I'm just… I'm tired of pretending. Tired of running from it."

"So what do you want from me?"

"I don't know." Her voice was small. "Maybe just… let's stop pretending we're okay when we're not. I failed you and Jason in the worst possible way."

Nick wiped his face with his free hand, surprised to find his cheeks wet. "I can't fix this for both of us, Mom. I can't make it better."

"I know. I'm not asking you to. But even if we can't fix it…" She paused. "Can we at least stop making it worse?"

The question lingered, demanding acknowledgment. Nick thought about all the unanswered calls, all the brief, surface visits, all the ways they'd danced around the truth for years.

"I don't know if I can see you right now," he said honestly.

"We're not going. Susan and I… we're staying in Paris. We're not ready. I'm not ready."

She sounded small, leaving Nick suddenly unmoored.

"Mom?" His voice came out younger than he intended.

"Yes?"

"I'm so tired."

"I know, my boy. So am I."

They sat in a different kind of quiet now, one that didn't cut the way other silent moments had.

"Maybe…" Nick started, then stopped. "Maybe we could talk again. Sometime."

"I'd like that." The relief in her voice was palpable. "Whatever you need, Nick. However slow you need to go."

"Okay." He took a shaky breath. "I should go."

"Nick? One more thing."

"What?"

"I love you. I've always loved you. Even when I failed you, even when I chose wrong, even when I was a terrible mother—I loved you."

He wanted to dismiss her words—lines delivered too late, too easily. But his throat closed up anyway.

"I know. That's what makes it so hard." A dozen years of lies stretched between them like a chasm, and now she wanted to build a bridge with nothing but apologies and promises as fragile as spider silk. He didn't trust her—not yet, maybe not ever—but the thought of seeing her, of hearing the whole truth, lodged itself in his mind and refused to let go. The questions he'd buried deep beneath layers of anger and hurt stirred to life. Nick thought of his apartment and the old photograph on his dresser, a snapshot he'd meant to throw away a hundred times but never could. In it, his mother smiled, her arms wrapped around his eight-year-old self at the beach. Before everything fell apart. Before the drinking, before her fights with Gene, before the summer he'd turned twelve. The memory of that day registered in him like a bruise—tender, but the sharp pain had faded to something duller, more manageable.

This thing with his mother felt unstable, like stepping onto thin ice, but even that could be something. Maybe he could stop running from the past, face his phantoms head-on instead of letting them haunt the edges of his life. The weight of unasked questions had become harder to carry than the risk of asking them. Gene's death had shown him that, if nothing else.

After a long pause, he made up his mind. He would meet her. Not to forgive, not to forget, but to listen—just enough to put some of the past to rest. Tomorrow. Somewhere public, somewhere neutral. A coffee shop in Saint-Germain, maybe, with a steady stream of customers and comfortable background noise. A place where neither of them could fall apart, where the presence of strangers might help them keep their composure.

It wasn't peace. It certainly wasn't closure. Theirs was a shaky step forward, or at least the shape of one. And maybe that's what healing looked like—not a dramatic reconciliation, but small, careful steps across uncertain ground, each foothold tested and prodded before moving on. He thought of the photograph again and noticed a shift. The memory no longer felt like a weapon to use against himself.

13.

The hotel room breathed around Susan as she slept on the far side of the bed, curled toward the wall, her exhales just audible beneath the hum of weather and midnight stillness.

At the window, Lynne sat cross-legged, phone in hand. The screen lit her face in cold, pale blue. She didn't blink.

After her call with Nick, she had opened Facebook. Not out of habit, not anymore, but out of something else. Something quieter. Like what Jason had described in the letter: times we can't understand and can't stop thinking about. Turning on a light, seeing everything that is happening in the dark, and wishing you could turn it off. The instinct that says *look again,* even when you already know what you'll find.

She typed, and the profile appeared instantly. Same soft-focus photo. Kate's sideways profile. She looked seconds from turning, like she would face the camera if you waited long enough.

Then the girls. Emma. Sarah.

Photos Lynne had seen before. Halloween costumes. School plays. Sunlit snapshots, limbs entwined. The ones with Gene were worse—bodies closer, always touching. Forced smiles, or none at all.

Lynne stopped at a photo from last winter. A frozen lake. The girls stood in coats too thin for the cold. Sarah looked straight into the camera. Her smile pulled wide, but her eyes stayed distant. The expression too old for her face.

Lynne's thumb hovered over the image, then drifted to the message icon.

She tapped it.

The blank field opened. The cursor blinked. She didn't type.

Excuses floated up: *Kate won't answer. It's not my place. What could I even say?*

And beneath these excuses, something heavier. Not fear. Not exactly. Something older. Grief that refused to settle. Guilt still wet at the edges.

The silence folded around her. The kind you wear because it's easier than telling the truth.

Her thumb trembled.

"I should..." she whispered.

She didn't finish the thought.

She could contact the girls another day. Or maybe, she never would. But first, she would hear Nick out, meet him at the café in Saint-Germain, undo—if only partially—the damage caused by years of silence and complacency. She locked the phone, setting it face down on the windowsill. The screen went dark.

14.

Carlos had been watching the whole time. Watching, waiting, listening. Nick didn't mind. In fact, Nick liked the idea of someone caring enough to stick around, even if out of courtesy or mild concern, if nothing more. Turning to Carlos, Nick's voice was low, almost lost.

"I used to dream about leaving Paris," Nick said. "About running somewhere new, yet again, becoming someone else. The way I left Missouri, the way I left banking." He mapped the pattern of shadows on the sheets, his fingers drifting between dark shapes, connecting invisible constellations. "But running would just mean more spaces to hide in. More walls to get trapped behind."

Carlos shifted and propped himself up on one elbow, his auburn eyes steady on Nick. The rain had slowed now, reduced to occasional drops hitting the window, punctuation marks at the end of a thought. He sat quiet for a moment, choosing his words, caught between empathy and something deeper, more personal.

"My son, Lucas, he's twelve now." Carlos's voice carried a mixture of pride and something more complicated—worry and wonder.

Twelve years old, the same age when Gene… Nick tensed, but didn't pull away. "What's he like?" Nick asked, surprising himself with genuine curiosity.

Carlos smiled. "Well, he's all questions lately. About everything. About me, especially." He paused, his hand smoothing wrinkles from the sheet between them. "He asks about the man I used to be, before I could be myself. Before I could really see myself. And I tell him…" He hesitated and licked his lips before continuing. "I tell him that person wasn't a lie, exactly.

Just... incomplete. Like waiting for someone to finish the story, you know? Last week, he asked me why I left his mother. Why I couldn't just pretend to be straight, keep our family together. Kids that age want everything explained, you know?"

Nick nodded, thinking of himself at twelve, desperate to decipher his hurt and confusion.

"What did you tell him?"

Carlos's voice grew quiet, thoughtful. "The truth. Or my version of it, anyway. I told him that sometimes the bravest thing you can do is stop pretending. That loving yourself doesn't mean you love other people less." He let out a soft laugh. "He said I sounded like his therapist."

"He's in therapy?"

"Started when I came out, when his mother and I separated. Her idea, actually. Probably the only thing we agreed on at the time." Carlos sat up and leaned against the headboard. "She was angry, of course. Felt betrayed. But she never used Lucas against me, never tried to keep him from me. I know how lucky that makes me."

Nick swallowed hard. "And Lucas? How did he handle it?"

"It was hard at first. He'd get quiet when I'd pick him up for our weekends. Wouldn't look at me directly. I thought... I thought maybe he hated me. That I'd ruined everything by being honest." He rubbed a hand over his face, collecting himself. "But then one day, he asked if he could redecorate his room at my place. Said if he was going to have two homes, he wanted them both to feel like his."

The rain had picked up again outside, a steady rhythm against the windows. Caught in the story, Nick found himself holding his breath.

"So we painted his room together," Carlos continued. "This awful electric blue he picked out—gave me a headache just looking at it. But we did it together, got paint everywhere, ordered pizza, made a whole weekend of it. And somewhere in the middle of it all, while we were sitting on newspapers eating margherita pizza with blue-stained hands, he looked at me and said, 'Papa, I'm glad you told the truth.'"

Tears pricked at the corners of Nick's eyes. He blinked them back, turned his face toward the window.

"The thing is," Carlos said, "I watch him so carefully now. Every move, every reaction. I'm terrified of messing up, of hurting him unintentionally. The other day, he wanted to talk about boys at school, and about a friend he thinks might be more than a friend. I caught myself wondering: Am I pushing him somehow? Making him think he has to be like me? Then I realized I was doing exactly what my own father did—questioning love instead of just letting it be what it is."

Carlos fell silent for a moment, lost in thought. "When Lucas stays over, I get so protective. Much more than I ever was when I was so-called 'straight' and living with my ex-wife. Every morning, first thing, I check on him. Just stand in the doorway and watch him breathe. It's ridiculous maybe, but I need to see him safe, to know he's okay. That I haven't broken anything essential in him by being who I am."

Nick twisted toward Carlos, his eyes tracing the other man's profile against the dim light. "That's not ridiculous."

"No?" Carlos met his gaze. "What would you call it then?"

"Love," Nick said, the word feeling strange on his tongue. "Real love. The kind that worries, that checks, that wants to protect." He swallowed hard. "Pretty much the opposite of what I had."

Carlos stretched out his hand and brushed a tear from Nick's cheek that Nick didn't even realize had fallen. "I think," he said, "that sometimes we learn how to love by recognizing what love isn't. By seeing the darkness and choosing to live in the light instead."

Nick's eyes fell shut as he leaned into Carlos's touch. "Does it get easier? The choosing?"

"Sometimes," Carlos said. "Some days I feel like I'm getting it right, like when Lucas calls just to tell me about his day, or when he falls asleep on the sofa watching movies, completely at ease. Other days..." He shook his head. "Other days I catch myself checking his room three, four times a night. Searching his face for signs I might have missed, hurts I might have caused without knowing."

"But you keep choosing," Nick said. "Keep trying."

"Every day," Carlos agreed. "Because the alternative—going back to pretending, to hiding—that would be its own kind of violence. And my son deserves better than a father who lives in the shadows."

They lay in the hush of time. Nick found himself thinking about Jason, about the different ways they'd both tried to escape their father. About how some people, like Carlos, chose to break cycles while others, like Gene, perpetuated them.

"Earlier," Nick said, "at the bar. When you were on the phone with Lucas. What were you really checking on?"

Carlos smiled, a small, sad grin. "He had a nightmare. Calls me sometimes when that happens, even if it's not my night with him. His mother allows it. Another kindness I probably don't deserve." He paused. "He was dreaming about losing me. About me disappearing. Kids that age, they carry so much fear beneath their questions."

Nick nodded. Understanding flooded through him. "That's why you seemed different after the call. More..."

"Human?" Carlos suggested. "Less like whatever you were looking for when you walked into that bar?"

The heat rose in Nick's cheeks, but Carlos's tone held no judgment.

"Yeah, I wasn't expecting... this. You," Nick admitted finally. "A father who cares about doing it right."

"Life's funny that way. Sometimes we find exactly what we need by looking for something else entirely." Carlos shifted closer, steady and present. "Want to hear about the time Lucas decided to become a professional magician? Spent three weeks practicing card tricks and made me sit through the world's longest magic show?"

The knot in Nick's chest eased just a fraction—not healing exactly, but maybe its shadow, the beginning of what healing might feel like.

"Yeah," he said. "I'd like that."

The weight of Carlos's words pulled Nick inward, into the labyrinth of his own thoughts. He thought about incompleteness. About all the versions of himself he'd tried to be—the perfect son everyone expected, the successful banker who never fit into his tailored suits, the designer living in curated stillness, the Parisian expat chasing some vague sense of freedom. Each version a mask that quickly expired, flawed and ill-fitting. He thought about Jason, trying to tell his truth through accusation and cryptic, coded letters. He thought about Laslo, painting in obsessive brushstrokes, desperate to pin reality to canvas and failing every time.

"This morning," Nick said, his voice tight, as though pulling the focus back to his own unrest, "I was so angry. Angry at... at everyone who saw and did nothing. Who pretended not to see what was right in front of them. But maybe… Maybe I am angry, yes, but also… were we all just trying to tell the same story in different ways? Maybe we were all just trying to make sense of something that never made sense."

Carlos reached out, his hand grazing Nick's—not a restraint or request, but a reminder of his steady presence.

Nick let his head fall back against the pillow, his chest rising and falling in a slow, peaceful rhythm. "I don't know," he said, almost to himself. "Maybe we don't stop running. Maybe we just learn how to carry the truth with us."

Carlos exhaled a slow, measured breath, as if testing the weight of Nick's words in the space between them. "We don't stop running," he echoed, his voice softer now. "But sometimes we think we have, for a little while. We think we've arrived. And then one day, we wake up, and it's there again—the thing we thought we left behind, catching up to us, slipping into the quiet spaces of our lives, reminding us that there's no such thing as arrival. Only motion. Only the next step."

Nick closed his eyes, listening to the distant city, to Carlos, to the hole inside himself that he had spent years trying to fill. He had thought Paris would be different—that the language, the streets, the anonymity would grant him a new beginning. But here too he measured his life in unfinished sentences, in moments that lingered too long. He thought of Jason's letter, of the truths folded between lines of grief, of Laslo's hands smudged with paint and frustration, and of himself, always watching, always searching, never knowing what he hoped to find.

Morning light crept in, pale gold against the bare walls. Carlos shifted, his gaze drifting toward the window. "Maybe it's not about carrying the truth. Maybe it's something we learn to live with. Something that irons out—softens—when we stop running from it."

Something settled deep in Nick's chest, a weight, a reckoning. He exhaled, feeling, for just a moment, the edges of something like stillness.

www.ingramcontent.com/pod-product-compliance
Lightning Source LLC
LaVergne TN
LVHW091143080826
845145LV00008B/2239

9781969935206